"Can you resist being wanted?" he asked

"Who wants me?" Yvain felt weak as water in the Marqués's arms. "I ran away from Kent in front of his friends, and Rique found out that we spent the night of the fog alone together... at least he found out that I was with a man."

"Did you not tell him I was that man?"

"How could I? The whole island would know and expect you...to marry me."

"If you don't agree to marry me, I'll see to it that the whole island *does* know. Because I want you. Because for me you are all the wonder of the world."

"But a marqués doesn't marry a maid," Yvain protested.

"This one does exactly what he wants to do," he said arrogantly.

VIOLET WINSPEAR
is also the author of these books in

Harlequin Presents Collection

Many of these titles are available at your local bookseller.

VIOLET WINSPEAR

pilgrim's castle

Originally published as Harlequin Presents #24

Harlequin Books

TORONTO • LONDON • LOS ANGELES • AMSTERDAM
SYDNEY • HAMBURG • PARIS • STOCKHOLM • ATHENS • TOKYO

Harlequin Presents edition published October 1973
ISBN 0-373-15016-4

Second printing August 1974
Third printing May 1976
Fourth printing September 1976
Fifth printing February 1977
Sixth printing March 1977
Seventh printing December 1978

This *Harlequin Presents Collection* edition published April 1981

Original hardcover edition published in 1969
by Mills & Boon Limited

CHAPTER ONE

SIRENS wailed, people screamed, and lifeboats splashed into the dark water. One of the boats overturned as it was being lowered from the tilting side of the doomed holiday ship, and Yvain Pilgrim felt a rush of night air and a sudden sickening dive into the sea. The water closed over her head, half choking her until she bobbed to the surface on the buoyancy of her life-jacket.

It was like a nightmare from which she couldn't escape. Her head was filled with the cries of people in distress, and yet at the same time she kept remembering the music to which the passengers had been dancing in the saloon. A sweet and sentimental tune, which had set her foot tapping and her heart yearning for a partner.

But no one had approached her as she sat quiet and bespectacled beside her employer, her hair in an unbecoming bun. Mrs. Sandell had been advised by her doctor to take a cruise in sunny waters, and she had cast an eye round her household and picked on Yvain to accompany her. Yvain had worked for the Sandell family since she was fifteen, first as a nursery maid and later as lady's maid and companion to the irritable Ida Sandell, who was well off and wrapped up in herself. The needs and longings of a girl of nineteen were beyond her grasp and her understanding.

From the outset of the voyage she had expected Yvain to be her constant companion. 'You're a sensible girl,' she said in her sharp, self-satisfied way, 'and you know your place. You mustn't expect to join in the fun and frolics of the other young people travelling on the ship, forever

5

swimming in the pool, flirting and dancing.'

Yvain harboured no dreams of a shipboard romance, but it would have been fun to play deck games with people her own age instead of reading Jane Austen to Mrs. Sandell. It would have made a delightful change to stroll the deck in the company of a young man.

But the plain little girl in the prim dress and spectacles did not attract the attention of any of the males on board the cruiser. They probably assumed that she was too shy, or too cowed by her large and formidable companion to be very exciting company. They had no idea that beneath her plain dresses and unbecoming cardigans there beat a warm young heart that yearned for adventure.

Adventure! Yvain felt drugged by the motion of the sea as she floated further all the time from the doomed holiday ship. Something had exploded down in the engine room. Water had flooded the ship in minutes, rushing in madly, and then the alarm sirens had swept the ship. All on deck! All take the places assigned to you! In the beginning Yvain had been next to Mrs. Sandell, no longer sure of herself but in a desperate panic, clutching her jewel-case and her handbag, and thrusting Yvain aside as a lifeboat was made ready. In the scramble Yvain had lost sight of her employer. When the lifeboat had overturned, she had heard a scream that might have belonged to Ida Sandell, cosseted all her life and now tossed into the sea that could be so cruel.

Yvain floated and remembered and was dazedly aware that there were no bobbing shapes to keep her company. The cries from the ship were dying away behind her and a dread silence seemed to enfold her. During the day the water had looked blue and warm, but right now it was cold and her limbs felt as if all the life was going out of them.

6

Sing out, she thought. Shout something. 'Ahoy!' Such a pathetic little cry in the silence of the night. 'Ahoy!'

No one answered. Nobody heard. Being so light she was being carried on the wings of her life-jacket out of hearing of the other passengers. Soon she would be entirely alone in the middle of the ocean between the rocky coast of Spain and the north coast of Africa.

It was a frightening realization. The loneliness of the past few years was made active by the loneliness of being adrift in strange waters. Her mind began to wander and memories of the past began to sweep over her . . . it was right what people said, when you were drowning you re-lived what had passed.

She came from a place in Somerset called Combe St. Blaize. There was a stone on the moors called the Black Angel, and as a child she used to play around it, gathering wild flowers to carry home to the cottage in which she lived with her gamekeeper father. Her mother had died when Yvain was born, and she loved the big, strapping, auburn-haired man who called her his squirrel and who cared for the game in the large park belonging to the Sandell family, up at the Hall.

She knew they were distantly related to the Sandells on her mother's side, and sometimes very early she heard the sound of hunting horns as the men and women of the family rode out across the moors after the red foxes. Because of the foxes Yvain hated the Sandells. They were big and florid and heartless, and she hoped she would never have to work for them as her father did.

Glorious Somerset. Summer land as he called it. There wasn't a moorland flower he didn't know by its name. Not a bird of the wilds that he couldn't imitate.

Yvain trembled in the water as she had trembled in the chapel the day her father was buried. So full of life, and then one awful day killed by a kick from the horse of one of the huntsmen, the warm burr in his voice stilled for ever.

Someone, a neighbour, had tied a big black bow in Yvain's hair — autumn-leaf hair, her father had called it, straight and fine as the rain in the woods.

There had been little comfort offered her after the burial, for she was but the orphan of a gamekeeper. No warm arms had been held out to her. Benumbed, the tears locked up inside her, she had been taken up to the Hall and put into a small room under the eaves, and the next day she had started work in the nursery, which was occupied by the two children belonging to Ida Sandell's son and his wife.

Everything had changed so fast, so confusingly. One day Yvain had been free to roam the moors, and the next she was taking orders from the Sandells. After a few months in the nursery, Ida had started to make use of her as a personal maid. Yvain remembered the Hunt Ball, a year after her father's death. The arrival of the week-end guests, the endless hours of arranging Ida's hair, of helping her to dress, of hearing the music as it floated up to the gallery where she sat on the steps to the attics and dreamed young and impossible dreams.

She might have escaped to a job in the city, but what did she know beyond carrying tea-trays, mending lingerie, walking Ida's corgi dogs, providing the novels she liked to read, and rubbing her feet as she lay on the chaise-longue?

She might have escaped . . . and now she had . . . drifting in a life-jacket, tossed like flotsam, cold and frightened with the darkness gathering closer and closer about her. Gone were the spectacles Ida Sandell had insisted she needed, and adrift had come her hair from its confining role at the nape of her neck. Her plain beige dress clung close to her slim body. She felt drowsy, like a child drifting on the edge of sleep.

Would it come soon, the sleep from which she would not awake? Would she see again the tall, vibrant figure who used to sweep her up into his arms and tell her that she'd be a princess in her own castle, like Rapunzel of the long hair that held the dark burning shades of autumn? Would it hurt, she wondered, as waves splashed over her and she heard in the night a throbbing that was surely the throbbing of her own heart, clamouring in her ears, growing louder until suddenly everything went as white as lightning and she was impaled on the beam.

Someone yelled out ... was it herself? More waves washed over her, choking her, and then there was a splash and steel hands seemed to seize hold of her. A voice spoke urgently in a language she could not understand. It was a man, holding her, and she clung to him as to a rock in the dark, churning water.

Some time later Yvain awoke to find herself tucked up in blankets in the berth of a small cabin. She lay bemused, feeling the motion of the boat, and a blessed warmth in her limbs that meant she was safe and very much alive.

Her eyes widened as the cabin door opened and a man entered. He wore a great jersey to his throat and his face was lean and olive-skinned. He came to the side of the berth and leaned over her, his dark eyes searching her face. *'Qué tal, niña?'*

She couldn't understand what he said, so she smiled at him. It was this young man who had pulled her out of the sea and saved her life. 'Thank you,' she said with deep gratitude.

He smiled back at her, then left her alone to rest from

her ordeal. He was nice, she thought drowsily. So big and stalwart, as though not even the elements could frighten him. He had a fine face, and she decided that her knight errant was Spanish.

The boat came to harbour just as dawn was breaking. A mug of steaming coffee was brought to Yvain, along with a roll-neck jersey and a pair of jeans with half the legs lopped off. By the time she had dressed in these garments, the sun was filtering through the porthole of the cabin and a glance outside showed Yvain that they were moored against the jetty of a shelving beach; the resinous tang in the air came from the tall pine trees that clustered above the beach.

She found her way up a narrow flight of steps to the deck of the boat, a small motor vessel bobbing against the stone jetty on which a girl had appeared. The dark fringes of her head shawl blew in the morning breezes, and she was gazing at the boat, from which Yvain's rescuer leapt with outflung arms. He and the girl clung together, and as Yvain watched them the old feeling of desolation swept over her.

She gave the couple several more minutes by themselves, then she walked to the side of the boat and was given a strong hand to the jetty. Her hair had dried and hung in a salt-bloomed tangle to her shoulder-blades. The borrowed jersey hung to her hips and she looked exactly what she was, an orphan of the storm.

The shawled young woman gazed at her with eyes big with curiosity, and like the young sailor she was olive-skinned and nice-looking. She broke into a smile when he said simply to Yvain: '*Mi mujer,* Mari Luz.'

Yvain understood him. Now her wits had cleared, some of the Spanish she had been learning with Ida Sandell returned to her. The pretty dark girl was the young man's wife. Yvain smiled half to herself. What a let-down to learn that her knight of the water was a happily married man!

She went with the couple to their white-walled house among the pine trees, where a curly-haired baby slept in a carved cradle, and where a fire of pine needles and chippings blazed cheerfully in the hearth. Mari Luz and her husband spoke together, then he excused himself and strode from the kitchen.

'*Telefona.*' His wife mimed the movements. '*El gran señor* to tell. *Telefona* at *lonja.*'

Lodge? Yvain stared at Mari Luz from the fireside as she began to lay the table. '*El gran señor?*' she queried.

'Emerito tell him of *la señorita Inglesa – comprende?*'

Yvain nodded. It seemed that Emerito was about to pass her on to some grand gentleman of these parts, but in the meantime she admired the baby in his cradle and ate the fried eggs and bacon that Mari Luz cooked for her. She was drinking a cup of coffee when Emerito returned and made her understand that a car was coming to take her to the house of *El Señor.*

'Where am I?' She gestured out of the window. 'What part of Spain is this?'

Mari Luz rocked her baby son in her arms and left her tall young husband to explain. In amazement, and some consternation, Yvain learned that she had been brought to an island off the coast of Spain. *La Isla del Leon* – The island of the Lion.

Even as she absorbed the amazing fact, there came the sound of a car pulling up outside the house. Emerito opened the door and Yvain went outside into the sunshine that was bursting through the trees and gleaming on the bodywork of the car that throbbed there. A limousine with a silver miniature of a lion mounted on the bonnet, and a crest on the doors. Yvain caught her breath. Even the Sandells had not driven about in cars like this one. Even they had not been important enough to merit a gold and scarlet coat of arms.

A chauffeur in a buff-coloured uniform emerged from behind the wheel and held open the passenger door. Yvain, an odd young figure in her sea-wear, smiled good-bye at Emerito and his young family. '*Mil gracias,*' she said. 'You saved my life and I . . . I can't thank you sufficiently.'

Emerito spread his hands with Latin eloquence. '*Dios te proteja, señorita.*'

God had protected her. She nodded, kissed the baby's soft curls, and slipped into the limousine. She sank back against the soft buff velour of the upholstery and was assailed by a sense of wonderment. Never had she, Yvain Pilgrim, dreamed of being swept to some fabulous domain in a chauffeur-driven car. There was even fitted carpet underfoot and a cushioned headrest against which she leaned her tousled head as the car drove smoothly off the forest path and turned to take a road that wound upwards.

The engine purred and Yvain was aware of a wild and wonderful scenery and the glitter of the sea that encircled the island of the Lion. Who was the Lion? Was it possible that she sat in his car and was being carried up and up to his *palacio*? She had heard that certain Spanish nobles still lived like feudal lords in these faraway parts, and Mari Luz had called the man who had summoned her *El gran señor.*

Suddenly Yvain's hand gripped the silver inside handle of the door beside her. She had an irrational stab of doubt and fear. She wanted to tell the driver to take her back to the kind young couple in their secure little cottage, but she had no real Spanish, she knew only a few words and phrases, and 'Stop the car, I want to jump out!' was not among them.

She gazed out of the window beside her and saw sheer cliffs, pine and gum trees, a touch of gold over the distant mountains, and an enticing blue to the sea.

The sea in which she had been plunged last night, so fearful then, now like a melting pot of sapphires and jasper. As she gazed far down at the water, as the car climbed with a deeper purr towards the summit of the hills, she wondered about her employer. Had Ida Sandell been picked up? Was she safe? Would she soon be making inquiries about her maid-of-all-work, Pilgrim, as she called Yvain?

Yvain was aware that she had an unusual first name. It came out of a book of fables, her father had told her long ago. Ida Sandell had sniffed scornfully at the idea of a maid-companion having such a fancy name. Pilgrim, she always called out when she wanted something. Fetch my book, Pilgrim. Massage the nape of my neck, Pilgrim. Take Jassy to the garden, Pilgrim, and see she doesn't go on the flower beds.

Yvain stared blindly from the window of the limousine. She didn't want to go on like some patient pilgrim, forever at the beck and call of a woman who thought only of her own comfort. A cruise in sunny waters had seemed exciting, but on board nothing had changed for Yvain . . . until the shrilling of the alarms, the tilting of the lifeboat, the plunge into the sea that had carried her near enough to the shores of this island to be picked up by a young Spanish sailor.

The Island of the Lion.

Her fingers gripped together in her lap, her gold-brown eyes slowly filled with wonderment. How could she forget the fable from which her name had been chosen by her father? Yvain, the girl who had been assisted by a lion in her fight against a dragon!

It was then, as the car stood poised on a precarious bend of the spiral road, that she saw etched against the sunlit sky the turrets of a castle out of a Spanish fable. She felt the excited drumming of her heart as she gazed upon the place. It was perched high on a ledge of rock, like a wondrous tapestry, its pinnacles soaring high to pierce the blue-gold sky. A pennant flew from a turret that seemed poised over the sea itself, and the gold and scarlet colours caught the wind and the sun.

Yvain let out her breath, very slowly. It was not a dream because she could feel the wind on her cheek, and she could smell the resinous pines and the salt in the air. It was not a dream, because now they were driving into the courtyard and Yvain saw a stone figure of a lion presiding over the entrance to the *castillo*.

The car circled a stone well in the centre of the courtyard and came to a smooth halt at the foot of a flight of steps leading up to an arcaded porch. The chauffeur slid from the car and opened the door beside Yvain. In something of a daze she alighted and stood gazing up the steps at the huge coat of arms dominating the porch. An escutcheon quartered into deeds of valour, pride, honour, and love.

She stared at the carved rose, symbol of love. She was entering the house of a Spaniard, of course, and it would be a place of warm affection, many children, and a smiling woman grown plump with contentment.

'*Por favor.*' The chauffeur gestured not at the steps but at a wrought-iron gate set in a wall of the courtyard. '*Permitir.*' He opened the gate, and Yvain entered a patio that made her catch her breath in wonderment. It was like walking into a picture, and she felt incongruous in her odd clothes among the rose-coloured trails of oleanders, the perfume of star-like flowers clustering about a fountain, and the wild tangle of roses cloaking a pergola.

'*Muchas flores!*' she gasped.

'*Si, señorita.*'

'*Un grand edificio,*' she added faintly.

A pair of dark eyes gazed amusedly into hers. '*El señor hidalgo es un hombre muy rico.*'

She didn't doubt the *hidalgo*'s riches, and she followed nervously where the chauffeur led, in through open glass doors, across a quiet, shady, gleaming hall, and up a gracious staircase of marble and wrought-iron.

The chauffeur paused in front of carved double doors and tapped upon one of the panels. He then took hold of the bronze handles and opened the doors and left Yvain to enter the room on her own.

Yvain stood just inside the doorway of the *sala,* trying to get her bearings, and aware of panelled ceiling murals lustrous as old jewels, gold-framed Spanish paintings against panelled walls, antique furniture, and silky rugs that echoed the colours in a mosaic picture of the Virgin and Child.

She took a step forward and at once the tall double doors were closed behind her and her eyes dilated as they settled on the tall figure who stood looking at her from one of the great arched windows. He was smoking a thin dark cigar with deliberate movements of his hand and she had an impression of aquiline features and cold brilliant eyes under brows intensely dark. His high cheekbones lent a satanic look to his face, and his dominant nose was matched by an imperious mouth. He stood unmoving against the stained-glass window, wrapped in silence and the incense of his cigar. A blade of ruby light played over thick black hair slashed with silver.

He was a grandee of Spain – imperious, aloof, sombre, dressed with an immaculate exactness that made Yvain desperately aware of her own odd garments, and the *alpargatas* tied on with cord around her ankles.

The *señor* appraised her in silence, from head to toe. Her fingers curled nervously against the sides of her loplegged jeans. She felt dazed by the grandeur of the man and his surroundings. She had not the nerve at this moment to tear open the door and run from the deep-set eyes and the chiselled mouth that looked as if it rarely smiled.

'You are the girl whom Emerito fished out of the ocean?'

'Yes.' Her heart was gripped by the alarm he aroused in her; she had known before he spoke that his voice would be deep and magnetic, but she had not known that he would speak English so perfectly and with the added edge of his Spanish accent. It was the voice of a dark sorcerer, compelling as his gaze.

'How are you called?'

'My . . . my name is Yvain Pilgrim, *señor*.'

'Be seated.' He gestured at a high-backed velvet chair. 'We will talk.'

She felt defenceless and was glad to sit down before her legs let her down. She was trembling. Never in her life before had she felt quite like this . . . this was surely fright at first sight!

He moved from the window that soared so high, and now she saw that he walked with the aid of a black stick and that his left leg seemed to have something amiss with it. When he reached the fireplace, over which his family crest was emblazoned, he gave her a slight bow. 'I am

Don Juan de Conques y Aranda, Marqués de Leon,' he said in that deep, spell-binding voice.

The impressive name made Yvain feel faint. So he was the Lion of the island ... feudal lord who ruled from his castle, and whose word was probably a law unto itself.

'We have a saying, Señorita Pilgrim. A Spaniard might wound you, but he will not immediately skin your hide. Stop looking so nervous of me!'

At once she was made even more nervous, for now he was closer to her and his almost black eyes were fixed upon her face, with its sensitive mouth untouched by any man's. The tapering cheekbones, the pointed chin, the tiny mole on her temple just above her wide-set eyes. 'Still waters run dangerous!' It had been a favourite saying of Ida Sandell's. And she had insisted that Yvain's hair be unbecomingly rolled up, and had further insisted that she wear the plain-rimmed spectacles prescribed for the slight difficulty Yvain had in seeing distant objects.

She had no difficulty in seeing Don Juan.

'Don't you like the look of my house, *señorita*? Many people find it beautiful with its sea tower, its almond groves, and its fountain courts.'

'Your house is a castle, *señor*.'

'My house is a castle,' he agreed sardonically. 'Have you never been inside one before?'

'No, *señor*.' She tilted her chin. 'What would a maid-companion be doing in a castle?'

'What indeed?' He fingered the roses in a golden bowl on the marble fireplace. Their scent mingled with that of his cigar. 'How many years have you, Señorita Pilgrim?'

She sat stunned, for it was not a question a man of her own nationality asked outright like that. He frowned and she realized that when the Marqués de Leon asked you a question, no matter how personal, you answered him without hesitation.

'I am nineteen, *señor*.'

'I thought you younger.' His eyes scanned her thin young figure, made waif-like by the clothes Emerito had provided. He drew away from the mantelpiece and limped to an exquisite little table on which stood a dish of grapes like drops of gold. He picked up the dish and handed it to Yvain. 'At the moment you look too young for wine.' A brief and faintly shattering smile touched his lips. 'Come, try them. They are from the vines of the *castillo*.'

The grapes were delicious, but Yvain felt shy of the dark eyes upon her as she ate three or four.

'Did Emerito feed you?' he asked, and now he stood in front of the mosaic picture of the Virgin and Child and he seemed to lean rather heavily on his stick. It struck Yvain that his leg pained him. His beautiful mouth seemed shadowed by pain, a hint of bitterness, something that made him a little less remote.

'His wife cooked breakfast for me, *señor*. I . . . I should have died but for Emerito.'

'Quite.' He studied her through his cigar smoke. 'It was the thing unbelievable, eh? A nightmare for you. Don't think about it any more. You are now safe—'

'All those people . . . crying out as the ship went down!'

'I expect many of them have survived, like yourself.'

'I was travelling with my employer, a Mrs. Sandell. I wonder—'

'If she is also safe?'

'Yes.' Yvain's eyes were wide with distress. She had never felt much affection for her employer, but she knew how it felt to be adrift in the dark ocean, with a numbness creeping to your heart.

'I shall see that inquiries are made.' His eyes narrowed as they dwelt on Yvain. 'You wish to return to her, if she has been picked up?'

'No!' The word escaped before Yvain could stop it.
'But I suppose I must ... I have nothing, no clothes, no
money.'

'Would you prefer to stay here?'

For a stunned moment Yvain couldn't believe that she
had heard him correctly, and then like the reverberation
from a bombshell it shook her that she had heard him all
too plainly. She stared at him, at a loss to understand the
invitation. He was a *marqués* and she was a plain and
bedraggled maid-companion ... was he, perhaps, offering
her a job as a maid at the castle?

'You ... you wish to employ me, *señor*?' she asked
faintly.

'My servants are all men except for my housekeeper.'
Again that brief smile flickered on his lips. 'No, *señorita*,
I am inviting you to stay here for a while.'

'But—'

'But what?' He raised a black eyebrow. 'You appear
none too eager to return to your former employment.
Would you not prefer to stay here at the *castillo*?'

'In ... what capacity?' She felt tortured, but she had to
ask.

'As my guest, Señorita Pilgrim.' His eyes held mockery.
'Did you imagine that you had aroused my passions?'

She blushed to the roots of her hair, and felt his eyes
following the course of that blush from her eartips to the
sea-tangled hair above her eyes.

'I assure you I don't exercise my *droit de seigneur* over
every female who sets foot on the island,' he said sardonically. 'To me you are but a waif on my hands. You will
stay here! I have made up my mind!'

Yvain sat speechless in the tall velvet chair, her hands
holding the dish of golden grapes as if they were an offer-

ing. What of his family? Surely they would not be pleased to have a waif landed on them for a guest?

'What now is the objection?' He leaned on his stick and studied her as if she were an odd little object, out of place in this beautiful room but with something about her that interested him.

'What will your family say?' she asked nervously.

'I have no family.' Suddenly his face was harsh, as if unwittingly she had probed a wound he kept hidden beneath his armour. 'I am unmarried and childless, *señorita*. There are cats about the *castillo* and an Alsatian wolfhound, but as you see,' he tapped his left foot with his stick, 'like Lucifer I limp.'

A coldness ran over Yvain. Lucifer the fallen angel, heaven denied to him because of having too much pride. Yes, she had thought from the moment of their meeting that there was something satanic about this man!

'You mean to be responsible for me?' she asked nervously.

'It will be a novelty.' He rang a silver bell to summon a member of his household. 'I realize that the English don't like to be under obligation to anyone, but the Isla del Leon is quite a long way from the mainland and you must accept my hospitality whether you want to or not.'

'I . . . think you kind to offer it, *señor*.'

'Kind?' His chiselled mouth scorned the word. 'I am practical and I am a Spaniard. My house is yours!'

Her glance stole round the *sala*, taking in the dark rich colours, glimmering rugs and golden rose bowl. She felt like the beggar-maid with King Cophetua!

'Everything necessary will be arranged with the *comisaria* on the mainland,' he said, and then he turned to the doors as they opened and a woman entered. She had a severe face and wore unrelieved black, and the

Marqués spoke rapidly to her in his chiselled Spanish. Yvain felt the woman's glance upon her and she met a pair of eyes that appraised her without warmth.

'*Si*, Don Juan.' The woman curtsied and withdrew from the room.

'My housekeeper has been told to prepare a room for you. Her name is Alma and you will find her quite helpful.'

Yvain looked at him in a lost way. He had taken charge of her as if she were a bedraggled kitten found on his doorstep, but there was not a glimmer of warmth in his manner. 'Thank you,' she murmured, and this time she didn't add that he was kind. She had the feeling that he wasn't moved to kindness by a plain little nobody like herself. He was curious about her and he invited her to stay here so he could study her reaction to his castle. She wished she dared oppose him, but reaction from her ordeal of last night was taking its toll of her and her eyes and limbs felt heavy and weary.

'From your bedroom you will have a view of the sea,' he said. '*O mar e lindo.*'

She winced to hear the sea called beautiful. She could not forget being adrift in its darkness, like flotsam. She could not forget her fear and loneliness.

'Do you understand our language?' Don Juan's eyes were fixed upon her and she knew they were reading her thoughts.

'A phrase here and there,' she said.

'Before you leave the Isla de Leon I daresay you will understand a lot more. And I, who knows? I may enjoy my guardianship.'

Devil guardian! The thought struck sharply and it brought Yvain to her feet. She clutched the dish of grapes and was reflected in her incongruous garments in a gold-framed mirror on the wall. She stared at herself, and then suddenly she began to laugh. The held-down hysteria welled up in her and she couldn't stop laughing, and even as she laughed the tears ran down her face. Through her tears the Marqués loomed over her, dark and forbidding, and then she cried out as he raised his hand and slapped her deliberately across the face.

'*Oh!*' A shudder ran all through her and her cheek stung. She stood like a child, tearful and slapped, and she hated the Marqués de Leon with all her young and lonely heart.

'We will have no more hysteria,' he said quietly. 'You will learn from this moment to have dignity, do you understand?'

'Why?' Tears spilled silently from her wide eyes. 'I . . . I told you I was only a maid to a s-spoiled and s-selfish woman.'

'You were a maid.' He caught at her chin and lifted her tear-wet face so he could study it, mercilessly. 'Yvain, you have an unusual name. You will live up to it.'

The fingers that gripped her chin were those that had stung her. He was cruel, beyond her understanding, and before he handed her over to his housekeeper he drew a handkerchief from his pocket and told her to wipe her foolish eyes. 'You will forget the sinking ship, understand? You will go and rest and tomorrow you will feel better.'

She wiped her eyes and felt utterly miserable. How nice to be one of those who in a crisis had someone with warm arms to hold one. How long ago it seemed since she had known what it was to be loved.

In silence she handed back the handkerchief, which he thrust into the pocket of his black velvet jacket. On his left hand he wore a heavy gold ring set with a single ruby.

22

The gem gleamed against the black. Satanic colours, well suited to a man such as Don Juan de Conques y Aranda, Marqués de Leon.

Yvain followed the housekeeper up a twisting staircase to her room, and she knew from the curving walls and windows that she had been put into a turret of the castle. The housekeeper opened an adjoining door and there was a bath tiled all over its exterior with gold and green *azulejos*.

'The *salon de aguas*,' said the housekeeper in her severe voice, and she showed Yvain which was the hot and which the cold tap, and opened a closet in which hung huge Turkish towels. A drawer beneath held soap, crystals and a sponge. Over in a corner stood a porcelain lavatory, and Yvain realized that she had complete privacy here in this turret suite.

She offered the housekeeper a smile, but the woman's features did not relax in return. Instead she flicked a look over Yvain's apparel, and Yvain remembered the snobbery of the servants at Sandell Hall.

'I . . . I think I shall take a bath,' she said.

The woman nodded and evidently understood her English. 'The *señorita* will find a robe and a nightgown on the bed. 'The Señor Marqués gave orders that clothes be brought from the town for the *señorita*.'

'There is a town?' Yvain exclaimed.

'But of course.' Alma raised her eyebrows. 'The *castillo* is isolated here by the sea, but six miles away there are shops, a hotel, and a theatre. There are large houses at Puerto de Leon. Friends of Don Juan have their residences there.'

Oh, what a relief to know that she wasn't entirely cut off from civilization! Yvain held a big bar of pine-oil

23

soap to her nose and sniffed the delicious scent. A bath, and a sleep in that big bed in the other room, and she would feel more like her old self.

'Would the *señorita* like some refreshment?'

'Would it . . . oh, would it be possible for me to have a cup of tea?'

'If the *señorita* wishes.' Again Yvain was treated to that faintly scornful look. 'We are not savages on this island. For many years a de Leon has been in charge of affairs here, and men such as the Señor Marqués are forward-looking.'

'He looks,' Yvain had to say it, 'as if he likes his own way.'

The housekeeper inclined her head with its smoothly coiled braids. 'A Spaniard is master in his own house, and Don Juan more than most. His family title and deeds are recorded in the history books of Spain, *señorita*.'

Yvain didn't doubt this statement for one second. The feudal history of the family was written on the man's face; was deep in his blood and bones. He could be generous, but she had already discovered that he could also be cruel.

'The island must be very beautiful,' she said, half desperately.

'The *señorita* will see for herself – come.' The housekeeper beckoned her to one of the windows, a casement which she opened outwards. At once Yvain could hear the sound of the sea, like the wind through the boughs of tall trees, sighing and restless; whispering a secret enticement.

'Lean out,' murmured Alma. 'Take a look.'

Yvain did as she was told and saw far below her the jade-blue sea and the turret-like rocks that it continually caressed, washing around them in foamy swirls. Yvain's hair blew in the salty air that careened about the turret in

24

which her room was situated. She felt like Rapunzel, held captive here by the dark sorcerer who was the master of the castle.

'The sea whispers.' The voice of the housekeeper was close to Yvain's ear. 'At night you will hear it and it will seem to belong to something human. You see, *señorita*, long ago a Leon bride was killed off those rocks.'

Yvain caught her breath and drew away from the window. She met the woman's dark eyes and saw their total lack of welcome; their intent to unnerve her.

'She was young, like yourself. She was from a foreign land, like yourself, and fond of taking for a walk along the cliffs of the castle a large wolfhound, such as the family have always liked to keep here. The dog pulled her by his lead to the edge of the cliffs, *señorita*, and they both went over.'

With these words the housekeeper walked to the door and opened it. 'When the *señorita* has bathed, I will fetch a pot of tea.'

The door closed behind her black-clad figure, and Yvain gave a cold little shiver as the sound of the sea and the wind entered through the casement, tangy with salt, sand and flowers. Haunted by a voice long silenced by the rocks and the waves.

For the first time she took a real look around her room and saw that it was quite beautiful ... like a room fashioned for someone who had come and gone ... or a woman who had never appeared to claim it. The bed was impossibly grand and covered by a lovely spread of lace, each petal and leaf perfectly detailed. The fine linen sheets were monogrammed, and a silver reading-lamp stood on the bedside table, carved from a brown-gold wood like the rest of the furniture. There were small silk-tapestry chairs and a matching lounger, and a deep carpet as azure as the sea, spreading from wall to panelled wall of rosewood.

Yvain could not help but compare it with her room at Sandell Hall, set beneath the eaves and furnished with cast-offs from grander rooms.

She heard, as in a dream, the pealing of nearby chapel bells mingling with the voice of the sea.

'There is a crossroads in your palm.' So had said the old Romany at the fair on the heath at Combe St. Blaize a week before she had left with Ida Sandell on the cruise which had ended so disastrously. She had wandered on alone through the fair, listening to the joyous laughter of other girls with their escorts, and in her heart she had hoped that the gipsy might say she was to meet her destiny on board the ship, in the shape of a tall, dark stranger. . . .

Yvain held her breath as she thought of the tall, dark, unsmiling stranger who had offered her a home for a while. He was not the young and charming man of her dreams . . . with his cold and finely sculptured face, his eyes that brooded and his leg that dragged, he frightened her.

He had mocked her for asking why he invited her to stay here . . . but what sort of feeling had she aroused in this man who lived alone in a castle by the sea?

CHAPTER TWO

YVAIN awoke to sunshine, so beckoning that in a moment she was out of bed and running to the casement window to take a look at her new surroundings. The nightdress fell half off her shoulders, being a couple of sizes too large, and she hung from the window with the awe of a child in her eyes.

Jade-blue sea, and distant mountains, those of Spain to which this island belonged. An island was like a world of its own, and now that a long sleep had rested her and beclouded some of the nightmare of the shipwreck, she felt an urge to explore her new domain.

She glanced about her turret bedroom and remembered what the housekeeper had said the day before, that clothes had been ordered for her from a store in the town that lay six miles away. The jersey and jeans of yesterday had disappeared, and on impulse Yvain ran to the big wardrobe and opened the doors. It was cavernous, and there inside hung a few dresses which she eagerly examined. An orange cotton, a striped linen, a flowered silky affair, and best of all a sea-green skirt and a starched frilled blouse with enormous puffed sleeves, a sort of peasant outfit to which she took a fancy. In a box with lilac flowers on it lay some under-garments, and Yvain lost no time having a wash and dressing herself in the skirt and blouse, after which she braided her hair and was about to pin it up in the old sedate way when she remembered that this was not Sandell Hall, nor the Marqués de Leon her former employer.

She allowed the braid to fall down in a soft rope over

her left shoulder, and her reflection in the mirror showed her a stranger to herself.

Without the disfiguring glasses her eyes were wide and inquiring. Clad in the short sea-green skirt and frilly blouse, with a wide belt to cinch her waist, she looked rather jolly. She grinned, and then remembered that Ida Sandell might not have survived the shipwreck.

She turned away from the mirror and decided to go downstairs in search of some breakfast. She felt famished, and put it down to the sea air which had drifted into her bedroom all through the night.

With a flounce of her skirt she ran down the twisting staircase set inside the turret, down and down until she reached a corridor that led right into the hall, and left beneath an arcade of a patio. The sunshine streamed through and she was caught and held by its gold as she stood in the archway, looking out at the scene.

There beneath a tree cloudy with mauve blossom was set a wicker table, and there at the table sat a figure with dark hair crisp with silver, absorbed in the peeling of a tangerine. Yvain was about to retreat when he glanced up, as if he sensed a presence, and slowly turned his head to look at her.

'Muy buenas,' he said. 'Please to join me, Señorita Pilgrim.'

She swallowed nervously, for though clad with some informality in a gold cashmere sweater over brown trousers, he still possessed a cool hauteur as he stood, one hand gripping the edge of the table, until she seated herself in the spare wicker chair. Again he sat down and she noticed how he stretched out his left leg, as if unable to bend it at the knee.

'You slept well?' He rang a silver bell and went on peeling the tangerine whose tang mingled with that of the flowers and plants festooning the walls of the patio.

'Yes, thank you.' Yvain felt shy and uncertain of him. 'I . . . I wondered if you had heard anything yet about the other people on the ship, *señor*?'

'Emerito has gone across to the mainland to make inquiries for me and, incidentally, to tell the authorities that you are staying here as my guest.'

It felt so strange to hear herself referred to as a guest when for the past few years she had had little leisure to relax and be treated as halfway human. She had waited on other people, not been waited on like this, for a man-servant had appeared and Don Juan was asking her what she fancied for breakfast. 'Eggs *flamenco*?' He quirked a black eyebrow. 'Warm new rolls, honey or marmalade?'

'Yes, please.' Colour stole under her cheekbones. 'It sounds delicious – and I would prefer honey.'

He turned to the manservant – who stood looking very polite and attentive in an immaculate white jacket over dark trousers – and spoke in crisp, rapid Spanish that added to the exotic surroundings in which Yvain found herself.

'I have had my breakfast.' Don Juan flicked a look over her frilled blouse and sea-green skirt. 'Coffee, rolls and fruit. I see that my wishes with regard to the clothes were carried out. This morning you look less like a wistful waif.'

'I am very grateful for the dresses, Don Juan. I . . . I can't think how I'm going to repay you.'

'I am sure we will find a way,' he said enigmatically, and she saw the hard glint of his teeth as he ate the tangerine. The sun slipped through the boughs of the mauve-flowering tree and warmed everything but the dark eyes that dwelt upon her. 'Life has changed for you in a very sudden and dramatic way, Señorita Pilgrim.

Does it not excite you that you stand on the threshold of new discoveries?'

'At the moment I feel rather bewildered.' She glanced about her at the Moresque tiling and arcades, old-gold walls and fluttering petals. There was a fountain, a hidden piping of birds in the pepper and oleander trees, a garden of beauty that yet could be hiding a serpent. It was all too dreamlike not to hold a dash of cold water, and Yvain was on the defensive. She had learned to be so, for even as music had played on the holiday ship, something had torn out its heart and pitched its defenceless passengers into deep water.

'You must learn not to dwell on what is past.' Don Juan spoke sternly. 'Believe me, *señorita*, memory can be too vivid an artist, but you are young enough to erase the dark colours for lighter ones.'

'At the moment it's all too vivid to be forgotten.' She touched a petal that had fallen to the table. 'I shall feel better when I hear that Mrs. Sandell is all right.'

'Yet you were not happy in this woman's employ?'

Yvain shook her head. 'She was a bit of a bully, but all the same – to drown!'

'We Spanish believe that every man or woman must fulfil what is destined for them. Ah, here comes Luis with your breakfast.' Don Juan rose to his feet and took hold of the silver-topped stick by his hand. 'I have affairs of business to see to, so I will leave you to amuse yourself. Explore, make friends with the animals, and if you wish for a book to read my housekeeper will show you the way to the library, which is situated in the sea-tower. Remember, you are not to paint your mind with dark pictures. Be young and carefree, for the day will come soon enough when you will no longer be free of care.'

He gave her a brief Latin bow, and she watched, her

fingers crushing the mauve petal, as he limped away and disappeared tall and dark into the cloistered hall of the castle. What had hurt him to make him a man who rarely smiled? Like his sea-tower he seemed aloof and wrapped in mystery.

Luis arranged dishes on the table in front of her; buttered eggs and warm crisp rolls, honey that glinted in a jar, and a silver pot of tea.

'*Gracias.*' She smiled at the manservant, but like Alma he was reserved, aware that she was unused to being treated like a lady. He flicked petals from the table and carried away the peel of the *señor's* tangerine. Yvain felt quietly snubbed. Don Juan had said: '*Mi casa es tu casa.*' But to his servants she was an intruder. They saw that she lacked the confidence of those born to giving orders and receiving service. They knew her for a lady's maid.

She was eating her breakfast when a large wolfish head came poking through a nearby curtain of flowers. The animal stared at her, then with a rattle of a medallion on his collar he came to investigate the stranger. She was quite unafraid of him, for there had been dogs galore at Sandell Hall. 'Hullo,' she said. 'I hope you're more friendly than the rest of your household.'

The Alsatian wolfhound sat down on his haunches and sniffed at her *torero* slippers with scarlet bows on them. He cocked his head consideringly, a cheeky-faced rogue with a ruff she could have buried her hands in. 'What's your name, eh?' She leaned forward and took a fearless look at his medallion. 'Carlos, shall we take a walk together?'

The dog gravely considered this, and then he shook the table as with a bound he took a look at what was left on the plates.

'Got to be bribed, eh?'

He gave her a yearning look and wasn't at all averse to roll and honey, after which he led her through an archway into the main part of the castle grounds. A flight of stone steps swooped downwards, with statues and pots ornamenting them at either side. Willow trees drooped over the statues and dappled them with green shadows, and at the foot of them stretched a water-walk, with sunshot arcs of water glittering against the green of the trees and the dazzle of many kinds of flowers.

Such a vast and wonderful garden for the pleasure of one man alone ... a place in which children might scamper and hide, climbing like squirrels up the many limbs of the magnolia trees.

She followed the dog's plume of a tail, along a path of strangely trimmed trees of a velvety foliage, meandering sunlit and shadowed to a domed glass-house. From the arched entrance hung a decorative lamp on a chain. She took a step inside and saw the down-curving fronds of palms and a shady interior set with wickerwork furniture and a pound in which goldfish gleamed in the undersea light. The fragrance of the orchids and the lotus-trees, from which tiny fruits hung, was heady. The sun filtered into the flower-house through the green glass of the dome.

Carlos poked his nose into the fish pond, and then flopped down on the cool border of gold-coloured tiles. Yvain glanced about her with delight, reaching for the cream cups of tropical blooms, and bending to open the bills of the colourful bird-of-paradise flowers.

Did Don Juan come here to smoke a nocturnal cigar, with the dog at his feet? Yvain could imagine him, lost in his smoke and the sea-green mystery of the place. A shadowy sculpture, the glow of his cigar illuminating his lean and brooding face.

She sat in a wicker chair and Carlos turned his head to

look at her. 'You're a bit of a lamb in wolf's fur, aren't you, Carlos?' She stroked him and looked thoughtful. How long did Don Juan expect her to stay at the castle? What would happen if Ida Sandell was safe and well and wanted her maid-companion?

Yvain breathed the exotic scents of the flowers that clustered and bloomed all around her, and she felt the peace and relaxation of not being at the beck and call of a woman as demanding as Mrs. Sandell. She could be carefree ... but she couldn't stop wondering what lay behind the Marqués' invitation. He was too cold and practical to be sentimental about a stray English girl.

'Did you think,' he had asked mockingly, 'that you had aroused my passions?'

Yvain bit her lip, and as if sensing her disquiet the wolfhound came and rested his head on her lap. 'Carlos,' she buried her fingers in his ruff, 'if only you could speak and tell me what your master is like behind his mask. He frightens me a little. He's like no one I've ever met before. The Sandells thought of themselves as gentry, but the Marqués de Leon is the real *nobleza*, and I can't imagine what he wants of me, a servant girl.'

The morning passed and she returned for a solitary lunch on the patio, after which everything fell quiet and she understood from Alma that her host would be absent for the remainder of the day.

'I would advise the *señorita* to take a siesta, otherwise the day will seem long. Don Juan will no doubt dine with his friend Señor Fonesca and his daughter the Doña Raquel at their residence in town, then they will proceed to the theatre. It will be late before he returns home.'

'The Doña Raquel has a lovely name,' Yvain said half curiously.

'I can assure the *señorita*,' the housekeeper's eye swept

over Yvain's girlish figure, 'that the Doña Raquel is a true Spanish beauty. When Don Juan marries, he could not choose a more suitable bride. A Spaniard of the nobility should love and marry a girl of birth and breeding, and he has the lesson of his own father's disastrous marriage to guard him from the danger of marrying beneath him.'

Yvain caught her breath. She wanted to ask questions, but with a rustle of black silk Alma swept on her way and left Yvain to ponder her mysterious, almost malicious words.

Late that night Yvain heard the return of his car as she lay in bed, sounding its horn for the gates of the courtyard to be opened by the keeper. She pictured the limousine as it purred through, its occupant in the back seat sitting dark and perhaps with half a smile on his lips as he thought of Doña Raquel.

There was a lot to be learned about the master of the *castillo* and Yvain hoped her stay would last long enough for her to discover what he was like behind his mask of cool, impenetrable reserve.

As it turned out it was several days before she saw him again. The castle was a rambling place and during the day she roamed about the grounds and explored its echoing rooms. When evening fell Don Juan either drove off in his car to dine with friends, or he took his evening meal alone, without inviting his young guest to join him. Yvain had the wolfhound to keep her company so she didn't mind being ignored. It made a change after Ida Sandell's persistent, 'Pilgrim, where are you? Don't go mooning off just as I need you.'

Then she learned from the housekeeper that Emerito had returned from the mainland, and all that day she felt keyed-up and it was no surprise when she received a message from the Marqués. She was to dine with him that evening at nine o'clock!

Her wardrobe did not include a dinner dress, so she had to wear the flowered silk. It was a size too large for her, but being well trained with the needle she was able to make it fairly presentable. The flowers were scarlet zinnias and they clashed vividly with her auburn hair, but she told herself Don Juan wasn't likely to notice what she looked like.

Came the moment to go down to him and after a final rueful glance in the mirror she slipped out of her room and descended slowly the stairs of the turret, a spiral about her slender figure, a background that intensified her youth and her uncertainty. She reached the hall, with its wells of shadow, its gleam of a panel, a picture, a suit of black and gold armour. In her *torero* slippers she crossed to Don Juan's private sanctum and her fingers trembled as she tapped upon one of the doors.

The hall clock chimed as she knocked. She braced herself and entered the room, and there he stood in front of a cabinet of beautiful curios, clad in a black velvet dinner-jacket over impeccable trousers, leaning on his stick and looking so distinguished that Yvain was stricken with shyness.

'Good evening, Señorita Pilgrim.' He spoke formally and looked her over without a change of expression in his dark eyes. 'We will go into dinner. The dining-room adjoins this one.'

With the assistance of his stick he walked to yet another set of panelled doors and opened them. Yvain preceded him into the dining-room, and its grandeur did nothing to dispel her shyness. The long table was set with candelabra and crystal, and the chairs, one at either end of the table, had a gilt coronet set in the head-rest. The manservant stepped forward and drew out the chair at

35

the foot of the table and Yvain slipped into it, her wide eyes collecting the candlelight as she looked along the table at her host. The coronet was above her auburn head and she looked as she felt, lost and insecure and rather afraid of the man who stared at her.

'We must see about getting you some well-fitting clothes.' His firm lips gave a twitch. 'And we will make sure none of them are scarlet.'

'But—' She took a deep breath. 'I shan't be staying here very long.'

'You think not?' He inclined his head as Luis hovered with a wine bottle. 'I have had some news today that may prolong your stay as my – guest.'

'News about Mrs. Sandell?' She half-noticed his pause before that last word, but was concerned about the woman who on more than one occasion had been unkind to her. 'Good news, *señor*?'

His lean fingers played with the stem of his wineglass as Luis came to her side with the wine. 'From the *comisaria* on the mainland I have had word that a Señora Sandell was among a group of passengers picked up and taken by ship to Tangiers. From there, I understand, she flew home to England by aeroplane, assuming no doubt that her maid-companion had perished. She could easily have found out otherwise if she had contacted the Spanish authorities, but it would seem that she could not be bothered. Having survived, she was concerned only with herself.'

Each word was as explicit and cold as a frost-etching on glass. The details were all too plain ... she had been abandoned to this man alone.

As she looked at him the candle flames bowed and were reflected in the polished surfaces of rosewood and silver. She tried to read his eyes beneath their heavy lids and black brows, and knew that she must bow to whatever he decided for her.

'*Salud.*' He raised his wine glass as if it were a ritual. 'You are no longer the maid-companion of a spoiled and selfish woman.'

The wine was chill and delicious, and though she was isolated from Don Juan by the glowing candelabra it was as if he reached out and took possession of her.

After dinner they did not return to the adjoining room. 'There is a small *sala* which is not used often these days, but I wish you to see it.' Don Juan's tall figure cast a long shadow and his ebony stick sounded on the tiles as he limped across the hall to a door guarded by a suit of Saracen armour; an oval door set deep like that of a sanctuary. He took a key-chain from his pocket and bent to unlock the door.

'This we call the *cuarto dorado*, the golden room,' he said, and as he switched on the light it was as if a jewel-box opened to reveal its hidden splendours.

'Please enter.' He waved her inside, and in a kind of dream she obeyed him and took in with wondering eyes the old-gold window drapes that swept from gilt crowns to the glow of antique rugs. She saw gracious furniture, golden bowls of roses, wonderful old frescoes, and panelling that held glimmers of gold.

It was a beautiful room, and forgetful of the dark man who struck a sombre note, Yvain wandered about touching lovely objects, such as a Moorish casket and an embroidered shawl thrown across a silent, unused piano of cream and gilt. A crimson rose lay on the shuttered lid; a haunted, romantic air of sadness hung about this room that must have been used often by a woman. Who had played the piano? Who had loved red roses and music?

Even as she turned to look at Don Juan, her eye was caught by a portrait and by a pair of shell-shaped castanets that hung on silk by the picture, which glowed against the panelling. Yvain took in the raven hair, the ruby-red dress, creamy-skinned face and flashing dark eyes. The girl portrayed stood in an attitude, her slender left arm thrown backwards, castanets on the fingers, the flowers in her hair as vivid as her eyes.

'That was La Rosalita.' Don Juan came and stood just behind Yvain, tall above her head, despite the fact that he leaned slightly on his stick. 'She was the gipsy dancer whom my father married.'

Yvain turned in surprise to look at him, and the breath caught in her throat as she met the full impact of his dark eyes, brilliant beneath his heavy lids.

'Yes, *señorita*, my mother was a gipsy girl, and my father's family never forgave him for marrying her. He brought her here to live, and made for her this golden room to which she escaped, during the time she was having her baby, to play on the piano the flamenco music she loved. She was all gaiety, all music, elemental as a flower that slowly withered in the atmosphere of frost which my father's people created for her.'

Don Juan's eyes dwelt with a faraway expression on the portrait of his gipsy mother. 'I can recall,' he murmured, 'how she would warm her finger-castanets in her masses of dark hair. Hair like midnight.'

He reached forward and took them from the hook on which they hung. He eased his fingers through the silk bands and their hollow click was like the echo of a broken cry. Then he replaced them and said they would take their coffee and *coñac* in here. He reached to the braided bell-pull, and Yvain studied him through her lashes and thought he had his mother's dark eyes and the kind of bone structure that denoted a fierce, hidden streak . . . a flame beneath the frost.

'Do you play?' He gestured at the piano.

'The duties of a maid-companion don't include such refinements, *señor*.' She spoke and looked demure as she sat in a silk-upholstered chair, her hands clasped in her lap. She wanted to hear more about his mother. Dared she ask? She thought not as he leaned on his stick in front of her and no doubt compared her in his mind to the golden girls of his own land.

'For how many years did you work for this woman?' he asked.

'Since I was fifteen, *señor*, when my father was killed by the kick of a horse.'

At once those black eyes upon her seemed to hold a flame. 'So! Was he out riding?'

'There was a hunting party at Sandell Hall and he was helping out in the stables.' Her hands clenched together with remembered pain. 'He was adjusting a stirrup when . . . when it happened. He loved animals, and yet that was how he died.'

'Your mother?'

'I don't remember her, *señor*. I had only my father, and then afterwards I worked at the Hall.'

'Secretly rebellious?' There was a tinge of sardonic humour in the question, and it seemed to Yvain that the beautiful, chiselled mouth was gentle for a fleeting moment.

'There were times when I thought of running away,' she admitted.

'Ah, then why did you stay?'

'Because cities are so noisy and when I could get away from the Hall for an hour I had the woods and wilds of Somerset to explore. I was close to the places my father always loved. There were the birds, and the Romany people camped on the heath . . .'

'You liked these Romany people?'

'They were colourful, but my father had been a game-keeper at the Hall, and so . . .'

Don Juan broke in with a laugh. It was the first time she had heard him laugh and her eyes reflected her amazement. 'Yes,' he said, 'there is an untamable streak in gipsies and they enjoy pheasant as well as the rich man.'

Luis entered with a coffee tray and was told to put it down on the table beside Yvain's chair. She felt the discreet flick of the manservant's eyes and she knew instantly what he was thinking. It was out of keeping for a little servant girl to be here in the golden room, the coffee set beside her so that she might pour for the Marqués.

Having been a servant she knew how they gossiped in the kitchen. It made her feel embarrassed that they might misconstrue Don Juan's attentions.

The door closed behind Luis. 'Please pour.' Don Juan took a chair and stretched forth his handicapped leg. He was intensely dark against the gold and crimson silk of the chair, and Yvain strove not to spill the coffee as she poured it from the silver pot, and she couldn't help but recall the number of times Ida Sandell had performed such a service for a male visitor to the Hall. Her hand shook slightly as she handed Don Juan his cup of coffee, in which at his request there was neither cream nor sugar.

'Are you nervous of me?' he asked.

'Can you wonder, *señor*?' She concentrated on sweetening her own coffee. 'I'm not used to . . . to all this.'

'I daresay practice will make perfect.'

She glanced up then as if a wire had jerked her to attention.

He quirked a black eyebrow as he drank his coffee.

'There will be other times, Señorita Pilgrim, when we shall be alone like this, and I hope that in time you will not look at me as if at the ogre of the castle.'

'I don't!'

'Ah, but you do.' His smile was mockery incarnate. 'You have a wide pair of eyes, *señorita*, and the eyes can be looked into as one looks in through the windows of a house that is otherwise locked up. It is an intrusion from the outside; a stolen glimpse into the soul of another person.'

Their glances interlocked and she felt indeed as if she surrendered to him a part of her secret self. *Bruno maga*, she thought. Dark sorcerer.

'Drink your coffee before it grows cold.' He rose with the help of his ebony stick and went across to crystal decanters on a tray with little silver lion's feet. 'This is an old bonded brandy,' he said as he poured. 'We will drink to your survival, and to your arrival on the Isla del Leon.'

His lean fingers held the goblets by their stems, and as she took one of them she felt its lightness. It was like an iridescent bubble with liquid gold inside.

'The world is small.' In his beautiful lean hand his goblet was like a chalice he held during some pagan rite. '*Un panuelo*, no more than a pocket handkerchief in the hand of chance. To chance, Señorita Pilgrim, the master of us all.'

A few moments after drinking the *coñac*, Yvain felt its soothing influence on her nerves. The room took on a glow, a warmth, and she could picture La Rosalita at the piano, a scarlet rose in her raven hair.

She saw that Don Juan was looking at the portrait, lost in his thoughts so that she was free to study his profile; the power and passion blended in the features, as silver blended with the darkness of his hair. Pain had left lines

41

beside his lips and silvered his hair, and she knew with her instincts rather than her eyes that he was a younger man than he appeared to be.

'Have you ever seen the flamenco dance?'

'No, *señor*. I have heard that it's very exciting.'

'The flamenco dance is a duel between a man and a woman.' The down swing of his glance caught her eyes upon him. 'I must arrange for you to see it. Spanish parents regard it as a form of education for their daughters, and I think there is much for you to learn.'

'I'm nineteen, *señor*!'

'The age of discovery. A step away from the teens to the twenties, when one is emotional without being in full command of the emotions.' His eyes were magnetic, holding her captive as he carried his dark *cigarro* to his lips. The black pearl studs in his shirtfront seemed to gleam like his eyes. 'You think me *arrogante*, eh? The know-it-all?'

'I think you regard people as chess pieces to be manipulated,' she rejoined, made daring by the *coñac*.

'And what chess piece are you, *señorita*?'

'I think ... the king's pawn,' she murmured.

'And what move do I intend to make with regard to you?'

'I can't imagine.'

'But I should have thought you had a lot of imagination.' His gaze dwelt on her hair, with its auburn shading to the brown-gold of her eyes. He appraised her in the dress that neither fitted nor flattered. He would smile, she thought, but he remained aloof, concealed behind a mask of suave, satanic beauty.

The word shook her as it came into her mind. One didn't apply it to a man, yet it had been applied ... to Dante ... to Byron ... to the martyred Sebastian. He was akin to them, this dark and dangerous lord of an island. This tall and limping Lucifer!

'Your imagination is at work right now.' He read her eyes and veiled his own behind the smoke of his *cigarro*. 'Our level of response to life is either deep or shallow, and our consequent torments arise from that level. I don't think you are shallow, Señorita Pilgrim, otherwise I should have asked Emerito to take you to the mainland.'

'I . . . I may have preferred to go to the mainland.' She felt a disturbing clamour of her heartbeats. 'I can't stay here indefinitely. I must find work . . . I have no money.'

'I have sufficient,' he drawled. 'I noticed at the dining table that you eat like a bird, and I daresay life has conditioned you to accept less than you secretly desire. What is your secret wish, *señorita*? I may be in a position to grant it.'

'I need a job,' she said nervously.

At once he smiled, an enigmatic twist of the lips. 'What an undemanding little creature you are! What sort of a job? Again as maid-of-all-work to a woman of no heart?'

'It's all I'm trained for, *señor*. Do you know someone . . .?'

'Ah yes, several ladies of leisure who would be delighted to have you for a runabout.'

'Then . . .?'

'I shall not recommend you to one of them.'

'Oh . . .!'

'Don't burst into tears!'

'I . . . I never cry,' she said with dignity, 'in front of others.'

'An admirable trait.'

'It would be to someone like you.'

'Like me?' There was a diabolical tilt to his left eyebrow.

'A Spanish aristocrat who has no need to depend on others for a livelihood.'

'In one way or another, *señorita*, we are all dependent on someone.' He traced with the ferrule of his stick the pattern on the silk rug at his feet. 'You must have the ambition to be something more than a maid-companion. Tell me, what would you like to do with your life?'

The fact that he showed interest, that he was prepared to be attentive, had the reverse effect of making her dumb with shyness. In any case she had never thought seriously about a career. One needed an education for that sort of thing and she had been taken out of school and set to work at the Hall when she was just fifteen. Of course, like every other girl, she had thought it would be fun to be an air stewardess, one who was whipped off to colourful lands in a streamlined jet aeroplane. And deep in her heart she had sometimes dreamed of being a smart assistant to someone brilliant in the world of art and antiques.

Yvain loved old and lovely things, and her response to this place was due to the wonders it held.

'Is your ambition so impossible that you dare not mention it?' There was a dry note in Don Juan's voice.

'You would only smile,' she said, at a loss to meet his quizzing eyes. Her gaze was upon the floor and it came as a shock when he leaned forward on his stick, took her chin in his hand and made her look at him. At his touch she gave a shiver she could not control. At that shiver a look of irony came into his eyes.

'I am one of those who will not be denied his way,' he said a trifle mockingly. 'Come, tell me your wish and we will see if I can make it come true.'

'You can't—'

'At least let me hear what it is I cannot do.' He held her face tilted up to him so that she was at the mercy of his

44

scrutiny. She couldn't escape him as he studied her country-girl skin, the slant of her cheekbones, her mouth that was wide but sensitive, her eyes that were a marigold colour. Hers was a face that wasn't at all pretty in the conventional sense ... but given the right sort of clothes and gaiety to light her features and she had the makings of an unusual attractiveness.

Yvain was quite unaware of this. She thought herself as plain as Ida Sandell had made her look.

'Tell me.' His eyes were magnetic, drawing forth the truth against her will.

'It would have been interesting ... to be assistant to a brilliant art dealer.' She gave a nervous laugh. 'But what could be more impossible a wish for me when all I know is how to fetch and carry and walk Madam's pet dogs?'

'You surprise me.' The pressure of his ring was against her skin. 'Young girls usually have a longing to be something glamorous, such as a model.'

'A model?' Her eyes were honeyed with laughter, and his eyes narrowed speculatively. '*Señor*, I am hardly the type for that sort of career.'

'You have unusual bone structure.' He turned her face from left to right, as if studying an *objet d'art*. 'So you would like to handle rare and priceless objects, eh? First you would have to know what makes them rare.'

'That is the drawback.' Her eyes took on a look of gravity. 'I have had no real teaching. I left school when I was fifteen.'

'Young lady,' his eyes were amused in a sardonic way, 'I was riding the plains of South America when I was a boy. I was a *gaucho*, as they call the cattle herders there.'

'But you are the Marqués de Leon!' she gasped.

'I was but a *gaucho* when I was fifteen.' His fingers slipped from her face, leaving a warmth she was very

45

conscious of. His gaze turned from her to that of his portrayed mother. 'My father died fighting in the Civil War, and my mother ran away from his family, taking me with her on a boat with other refugees bound for Argentina. There she worked as a flamenca dancer, and there I grew up to become a *vaquero*, until driven by ambition I set off to mine for silver in the hinterland. I had luck, I found a silver mine, and I bought a house for my mother in Lima and there she lived, without any more need to dance for the toughs that frequented the cafés.

'She died of sadness of the heart, *señorita*, and in the course of time my grandfather also died and I returned to the Isla del Leon. I have never forgiven the slight to my mother. My father's family wanted me but not Rosalita, and I chose to stay with her and to find my own education. Events conspired to bring me back to the island, but I left behind me an affection for Lima, with its savage history and its strange beauty.'

His eyes flashed to meet Yvain's. 'Yes, the *vaquero* lives in the saddle,' he said crisply. 'I was not always as you see me now.'

'You . . . had an accident, *señor*?'

'Yes, an accident.' He seemed not to want to discuss that aspect of his life in Lima, and for a moment his features were drawn with a harsh memory. 'So you wish to work among old and lovely things, eh?'

'It's nice to dream,' she said with half a smile.

'It need not remain a dream. You are not a shallow young person. I can see for myself that you have an appreciation of this room with its antiques from Lima and its carved furniture. Of course you need to learn a lot of things, and a couple of foreign languages are necessary. There resides on the island a friend of mine who knows a great deal about the lives of great painters and

46

sculptors, and who in his younger days was a teacher of languages. A Señor Fonesca – ah, do you know of him?'

'Yes, *señor*.' She thought of the housekeeper's words, that Señor Fonesca had a daughter of great beauty whom Don Juan would probably make his wife.

'Good. I will take you soon to meet him and we will discuss the possibility of your becoming his pupil for a few hours each day – you widen the eyes in amazement. Is this not what you would like, to receive education from a man of learning?'

'I . . . I'm thinking of the cost, *señor*.'

'Then stop thinking of it, instantly.' His dark eyes held hers, brilliant and yet inscrutable. 'The day may come when you can repay me. In the meantime it will amuse me to be the guardian of an English girl.'

'Guardian?' she faltered.

'Did we not agree that I would be responsible for you while you reside on the Isla del Leon? If Señor Fonesca agrees to accept you as a pupil, then it will be some time before you are ready to leave the island for the world of art and antiques. You need a home, so you will stay here. I have a relation on the mainland, a Doña Augusta, who can come and be your *duenna*. There,' his smile was mocking, 'will that satisfy your sense of propriety?'

She flushed and found it disconcerting the way he could read her mind. 'I . . . don't know how to thank you, Don Juan.'

'I shall be quite rewarded if one day I walk into an art gallery and find Yvain Pilgrim in charge.'

Even as he spoke he looked her over. 'Tomorrow you will request of the housekeeper that she takes your measurements. They will be sent to the fashion house of Ignazio in Madrid, along with details of your colouring, and half a dozen pairs of everything will be ordered, including day and evening dresses suitable for the life you will now lead as my ward. And,' he held up a hand as if to restrain the words on her lips, 'you will not mention another word about being grateful. I do this for my own sake. The red flowers on that dress do not accord with the colour of your hair, *señorita*.'

She might in that moment have warmed to him, for she was deeply grateful for the chance he was giving her, but he limped past her to the door and opened it. 'You will now go to bed,' he said.

She slipped past him into the hall. 'Goodnight, *señor*.'

'*Buenos noches*, Señorita Pilgrim.' He gave her a bow that was dismissive, and feeling chilled again she hastened away and heard the door of the golden room close behind him.

Forever, and forever life had changed for her. Her devil guardian had granted her wish and she was going to train for a career.

There was no one about in the hall and she did a jig and curtsied to her reflection in a wall mirror. 'You are going to learn how to be a lady, Miss Pilgrim.' She smiled at the country burr in her voice. 'There now, you never thought that would happen, did you?'

On her way up the turret stairs she thought of Ida Sandell, who hadn't cared enough to inquire if she had been picked up by a boat and brought to safety. Just as well Ida hadn't asked; she would probably have demanded the return of her maid-of-all-work, and Don Juan would not have said that from now on she would be his ward.

CHAPTER THREE

IT was impossible to sleep late at the castle, for the sun was an early invader, filling her turret room with warmth and light. She would quickly wash and dress and make her way down to the beach, postponing breakfast in order to avoid being alone with Don Juan. After his coffee and fruit he went to his sea-tower to work, or he ordered the car to be brought round to take him to a business meeting in town.

He was very much involved in all that concerned the island, and was a director on the board of several companies that maintained work, education and the health of the people. But Yvain had no idea what occupied him in the sea-tower, a place that fascinated her, but one she had not yet dared to explore, though he had given her permission to use the library there.

She could have asked the housekeeper, but since the morning Alma had taken her measurements and they had been sent to the famous fashion house in Madrid, there had been a tight-lipped, frozen air about the woman, as if she thought Don Juan's prodigy a little gold-digger.

Yvain plucked a wild oleander as she made her way down the path to the shore. She would have been happy to make do with the simple clothes she had, but Don Juan was a fastidious man, and having decided to look upon her as his ward, he didn't wish his critical eye to be offended by a badly dressed girl.

She tucked the flower in her braid and stood looking at the sea that creamed to meet the gold of the sands. How incredible that all this blue and sparkling water had

49

seemed one dark night as if it would drag her down and choke her. Even yet the fear lingered and though she played about on the beach, collecting shells and enjoying a game of ducks and drakes with pieces of driftwood, she did not venture into the water for more than a paddle. She had no desire to learn how to swim since the night of the shipwreck.

There was a bark and Carlos the wolfhound came dashing along the beach to join her in a game. She threw smooth pieces of driftwood for him to chase after, and soon they had drawn near to the path that led to Emerito's cottage in the woods. She decided to visit Mari Luz and the baby, and was only too willing to stay to breakfast and later to mind the *niño* while Mari Luz went off on the donkey to do some shopping at the little fishing village a mile or so further along the shore.

Having worked for a year in the nursery at Sandell Hall, Yvain was adept at amusing small children. Everything was sunshine until the *niño* picked up a shiny pebble in his chubby fist and thrust it into his mouth. Yvain lost no time removing it, and this set him off howling. He howled so lustily that Carlos joined in, and Yvain was pacing the sands, trying to pacify the little eater of stones, when someone appeared on the beach and stood taking in the scene with amused dark eyes.

Suddenly there drifted to Yvain's ears the music of a guitar and she glanced round to see a young man strolling towards her. As she drew nearer he began to sing a Spanish song in a voice that was as velvety as his eyes. He wore matador trousers and a thin silk shirt and a red scarf fluttered at his throat. He was young and black-haired, and as he serenaded the girl and baby he leaned against a tree, and as if by magic the baby stopped crying and lay sucking his thumb with contentment.

50

The young man sang and played until the *niño* slept, and then with a soft litheness he came forward and took a look at the beatific infant in Yvain's arms.

'*Mil gracias, señor*,' she said shyly.

He replied in Spanish, but she didn't understand a word he said. 'I'm sorry,' she looked up at him and was very aware of his Latin good looks, 'I'm afraid I don't speak Spanish.'

'Ah!' A gleam came into his eyes. 'Your baby has a lusty pair of lungs, *señora*. He will be a singer like me, eh?'

She smiled at his very natural mistake. 'The baby isn't mine, *señor*. I'm minding him while his mother goes shopping.'

'I see.' That gleam in his eyes became a sparkle. 'When I see you just now, I think to myself, Rique, again it is your misfortune to arrive too late! Such hair, like that of the Madonna. And like the Madonna a mother. But no! After all it was a glad mistake ... you are not, *señorita*, the possession of some other man?'

'No, I'm not,' she said breathlessly, and she just had to escape for a moment from his exciting eyes. She laid the *niño* on his striped blanket, and when she again looked at the young guitarist he gave her a Latin bow and introduced himself as Manrique Cortez y Esteban, a resident on the island for the six weeks he was engaged to appear as singer at the Club Hidalgo in Puerto de Leon.

'You permit me to sit beside you?' He gestured at the sand and the next moment he sprawled there at his ease and looked at her with a waiting smile. At last he said amusedly: 'Will the *señorita* not tell me her name? We might speak for an hour and then part, but if I know your name I shall be able to find you again.'

'Would you want to?' She had never flirted with a man in her life before and was amazed at how easy he made it.

'With some an hour is enough in which to learn everything, with others it might take a lifetime.' His eyes dwelt on her hair in a soft rope down over her slim shoulder. 'You should have a name that is not modern, for there is something unusual about you. You are different from the gay young holidaymakers I have met and spoken with in Spain.'

'You speak excellent English, *señor*.'

'You are English, *señorita*?'

'Of course.'

'There is something about your voice that is different — to tell the truth.' His teeth flashed in a smile. 'I am very intrigued by you.'

It was a flattering statement and Yvain, with amusement, couldn't help wondering what this young Lothario would have made of her in one of her shapeless beige dresses with her hair in a bun and a pair of plain-rimmed spectacles perched on her nose.

He leaned slightly forward to study the smile on her lips, but she felt no fear, none of the wild urge to retreat, as she did with Don Juan.

'Even your smile is mysterious,' he murmured. 'Have you come from some place of enchantment in those pine-woods?'

'Perhaps a castle,' she teased. 'With my hound to guard me.'

'Yes.' He eyed Carlos, whose large, fur-ruffed head was close to Yvain's shoulder. 'What a creature to fall out with. Are you not afraid of him?'

'Not in the least.' She gave Carlos a fond caress. 'He's really a lamb.'

'He looks like a wolf.'

'Supposing I said the same about you, *señor*?'

'*Touché!*' He laughed, with enough appreciation of the

quip to give away the fact that he was fond of a flirtation. 'The Spanish are a warm-blooded race of people, *señorita*, with a taste for intrigue and romance. No Spaniard is cold, you know. The good *Dios* gave him eyes, feelings, a strong pair of arms, and whether a Latin man is young or old he uses them.'

'Isn't that a little difficult, with an iron grille between a Spanish couple?' Her smile was deceptively demure.

'There is no such barrier between us,' he said wickedly.

'There is Carlos, and the fact that I hardly know you, Señor Cortez.'

'That is a promising remark, Señorita Mystery. Dare I hope that you are going to allow us to become – friends?'

'It's always nice to have friends.'

'A girl so attractive must have several.'

'On the contrary,' her fingers were lost in the dog's ruff, 'there is only Emerito and his wife. I . . . I can't be certain about the Marqués de Leon.'

The young guitarist raised his eyebrows. 'You know the Marqués?'

'Who can be said to know him?' Her eyes brooded on the blue sea that surrounded the Island of the Lion. 'I live with him . . . oh dear, that sounds very scandalous! I am his ward, *señor*.'

'His ward? You mean – you are the girl who was picked up from that holiday ship? Why, everyone in Puerto de Leon is talking about you. They are all very curious, but the Marqués is a man whom no one dares to question. So – he calls you his ward.'

'Yes!' She jumped to her feet, startling the dog and bringing a whimper from the baby of Mari Luz. 'What is everyone saying, Señor Cortez, that I am a gold-digger?'

'You?' He rose with lithe grace to his feet and stood head and shoulders above her, the silk of his shirt flattening against his hard young body as a breeze blew in from the sea. 'How could anyone look at you and think such a thing? Besides, the Marqués de Leon is no one's fool. He has a reputation for generosity, but no woman – so it is said – has ever turned his heart.'

'He's a Spaniard to his bones,' she rejoined. 'Are not Latin men warm-blooded, whether young or mature?'

'I was talking about ordinary men.'

'Yes, I suppose you were.' Their eyes met and held in the sunlight. 'Emerito, who works for him, found me in the sea and brought me to the island. The Marqués said I was to stay at the castle until we heard whether my employer was safe. She was, but she left me stranded. . . I have no one but Don Juan. He's kind to me in his own way.'

'Have you never thought that he has a significant name, *señorita*?'

'You said that no woman . . .'

'The other Don Juan broke hearts though his own remained intact.'

'You think my heart is in danger?'

'The Marqués is a distinguished man.'

'And I was a maid until two weeks ago, Señor Cortez.'

'Will you not be kind and call me Rique?'

'You still wish to be friends with me, *señor*?'

'More than ever.' He smiled in his beguiling way. 'If you won't tell me your name, then I shall call you La Soledad.'

'What a sad name!'

'It means girl of loneliness, a condition I mean to change.'

'You are very sure of yourself!'

'Don't you wish to be pried out of your shell?'

'It sounds a painful process—'

'I promise you it won't be painful at all.' His hand

moved as if he would fondle her braid, but he only took the flower that clung to her autumn-leaf hair. 'Life is like the oleander, a mixture of sweet and bitter. We will meet again, La Soledad. *Hasta la vista.*'

He went as he had come, silently among the trees, but a few moments later Yvain heard the motor of a fast car and she imagined it ripping away in the wind, the red scarf at the young man's throat a thread of colour until he was quite out of sight.

She picked up the baby and the blanket and made her way to the cottage. Mari Luz had returned and brought with her some enormous golden melons. The two girls had coffee together and when Yvain said that it was time for her to go, Mari Luz insisted upon giving her a melon. It was so plump and such a lovely colour that Yvain couldn't resist the present, and so it was that she arrived back at the castle with the melon in her arm and a smile on her lips.

She entered through the wrought-iron *cancela* of a patio, and was immediately startled to find Don Juan in occupation . . . and in the company of a startling beauty in a cloudy lavender chiffon dress and a shady hat that yet revealed the creamy face and large dark eyes beneath the transparent brim.

Yvain stood by the *cancela*, holding the melon and wildly wishful that it was large enough to conceal her tousled, sandy-legged, sun-hot figure from the elegant couple who sat in conversation beneath a Paradise-tree whose blossom was the same colour as the girl's dress.

Don Juan slowly glanced up and for an endless moment his dark eyes seemed to capture Yvain in all her youthful inelegance. He wore an immaculate white suit, and his thick hair had the gleam of a raven-wing.

With that polished politeness of his, and the merest

flick of amusement in his eyes, he rose to his feet with the aid of his ebony stick and greeted Yvain. 'Please come and meet Doña Raquel Fonesca,' he said. 'I have been telling her about my plan to have you become a student of her father's.'

Yvain – still clutching the melon – came forward obediently and felt her person and her cotton dress sized up by a pair of alluring eyes.

'How nice, Miss Pilgrim, to have the delight of meeting you.' Doña Raquel had the warm voice of coquetry, and her accent was charming. Her laughter held a breathless note as she turned to look at the Marqués.

'Juan, you did not tell me that your ward was such a child of nature! How touching – with the melon and all. Now I understand why you wished to take her under your providential wing.'

He inclined his head as if in agreement with every word that came from those silky red lips ... words that jarred on Yvain, with their undercurrent of mockery. Melon and all! She wanted to toss it behind the bushes, but when she remembered Mari Luz and her pleasure in giving the fruit, she felt ashamed of herself for caring what this self-assured rich girl thought of her and her melon.

'I'm looking forward to meeting Señor Fonesca,' she said, a tilt to her chin. 'I understand from the Señor Marqués that your father is a man of learning and culture.'

It was a deliberate attempt at a come-back, and Yvain felt beside her the stiffening of Don Juan's immaculate figure. 'Doña Raquel is staying to lunch at the castle,' he said frigidly. 'You have half an hour, Yvain, in which to make yourself presentable.'

'You wish me to join you?' Yvain had harboured the hope that she would be spared the ordeal of sitting at table with the Latin girl, whose dress was lovely, whose make-up was perfect, whose hair was not bloomed by the salty air of the beach.

'That is my wish,' he rejoined, and Yvain caught the smile that curved on the lips of Doña Raquel.

'Your wish is your ward's command, eh, Juan?' And she pronounced his name with perfection — caressing it almost.

'I'll go and get ready. Please excuse me.' Yvain almost ran from her guardian and his guest, her fingernails stabbing the melon which she threw on to the bed when she reached her room. She stared at herself in the mirror of the wardrobe — she looked a *gamine*, a grubby little ward of charity. Was it any wonder that Raquel Fonesca should think her an amusing target for a few sly digs?

She opened the wardrobe and took out the leaf-green skirt and blouse with the frilly sleeves, and as she washed and dressed she wondered when her new clothes would arrive from Madrid. At first she had felt reluctant about accepting them, but now she was glad they had been ordered for her. As the ward of Don Juan she would have to meet his friends, and he didn't wish to be embarrassed by her, nor did she wish to be hurt by girls who had never known what it was like to be an orphan, and then a maid who was on her feet from daybreak to bedtime.

It was a very gay luncheon on the part of Doña Raquel, who was well versed in all the tricks of charming a Spaniard. She was coquettish and demure by turns, and it seemed to Yvain that her aloof guardian was enchanted by her. He listened to her with a smile on his lips, and even laughed when she described the party she had attended on board the yacht of a celebrated matador.

'He wore diamond cuff-links, Juan, and said that next time I visited Seville I was to see him fight in the bull-ring and he would present the ear to me.'

'How horrible!' The words escaped from Yvain before she could stop them. 'I mean – about the bull, not the cuff-links!'

Doña Raquel gave her a cool look, her fork poised above the rich sweet on her plate. 'It is ironical that the British should think us cruel because of the bullfight. Is it not a fact that your countrymen go hunting in red coats? I believe their quarry is the fox or the stag?'

'I hate hunting as well.' Yvain's face had gone white, for inevitably she was reminded of the sound of horns on a misty morning, and of her father's death in the stables at Sandell Hall. 'People who think it sport to bait others never feel anything but the thrill of being cruel, and I wish my country would outlaw hunting.'

'The bullfight is a contemptible spectacle.' Don Juan spoke quietly but with an edge to his voice. 'I have always hated the masking of the picadors' horses.'

'You say that, Juan, when it was a horse—'

'We will not discuss it, Raquel.' He smiled, Yvain noticed, but his eyes were as still and dark as pools whose depths could be hiding many mysteries. 'There is to be a concert at the Club Hidalgo. I should think my ward would enjoy it, eh?'

Doña Raquel gazed across the table at Yvain in her peasant-type dress, with her hair in a braid and her slim young neck bare of adornment. The Spanish girl fingered her own glowing pearls and said demurely, 'Are you sure Miss Pilgrim will like our music, Juan? It is rather different from the guitar strumming of the pop groups in her own country.'

He looked at Yvain, and his lean fingers played with the stem of his wine glass. 'Are you a fan of pop music?' he asked her.

'I never really had the time to find out, *señor*,' she replied. 'Now and again there were dances at the Hall and an orchestra was hired for the occasion, but my employer's friends were not exactly the jet set.'

He smiled, and for a bewildering moment it was as if she entered his dark, dark eyes and found there a promise of sympathy, even of humour.

'I think we can rest assured, Raquel,' he said, 'that my ward has not yet lost her innocent values. The guitar playing of Manrique Cortez will not be lost upon her.'

Yvain's heart seemed to miss a beat. So – in the company of Don Juan – she was to see again the young man who had called her La Soledad, the girl of loneliness. The prospect was exciting!

CHAPTER FOUR

THE flower-house was like a grotto of shade and scent, with tiny stabs of golden sunlight revealing a scarlet zinnia, a palmetto, or a little lantern fruit on a lotus-tree. It was Yvain's hideaway, where she read a book or just enjoyed being lazy. In her heart she waited impatiently for the moment when the Marqués would take her to meet Señor Fonesca. She looked forward to becoming a student, and longed to learn about art and literature and all the things that would enable her to start a career.

If romance ever invaded her thoughts, it took a nebulous shape. It would be nice, she thought, to be loved and protected with passion, but the man who was to do this was only a dreamlike figure. He might never emerge as a reality, or as someone who could love her in return, but a career meant bread and butter, an interest in life, and being someone in her own right.

'I'm like Galatea,' she would sometimes reflect. 'Or Eliza Dolittle.'

The latter thought made her smile, for Don Juan was no crusty professor. He was a Spanish grandee who had made her his ward because it amused him.

She took walks along the cliffs above the little fishing harbour, and found starfish and medusa on the beach when the tide was out. Crabs scuttled beneath borrowed shells, and seaweed cast wet, soft traps about her bare feet. The little village was called San Cáliz, and she would watch the fishermen hauling in their nets, and wander along cobbled streets roofed with arcades and out again into the dazzling sunlight.

The smoke from wood fires hung on the air, and there was windmill irrigation that added to the legendary air of this island. It lay hidden from the world, and there was the ruin of an old monastery on a bluff where long ago the monks had defended the islanders with cannon when the sails of pirate ships were sighted.

All of this had an appeal for Yvain. She had never been a city girl and she revelled in the sands as she ran along them, her hair flying out behind her, her gaze upon the castle, standing there on the cliffs like something out of a dream with its curving walls and its crowned turrets, and its sea-tower whose narrow windows gleamed golden with light.

Don Juan was up there, the master of her castle of refuge, a subtle, dominant, aloof man who liked to give the impression that he had no sentimental feelings. Yvain wondered if he had been hurt out in Lima. The other day horses had been mentioned and he had changed the subject. He had received his injury while out riding ... was that the reason the stables at the castle were empty and echoing?

Yvain arrived back at the castle that afternoon to find that in her absence the Magi had arrived with gifts and gone silently away again. Long, square and rotund boxes were piled on the end of her bed and on the chairs, and she tore off seals and wrappings in her eagerness to see their contents.

Her hands were lost in filmy things of white and palest apple-green, exquisite lingerie in a silvery box. Her fingers stroked dresses of jersey-silk and pleated chiffon; evening gowns of lustrous velvet; beachwear, and simple day dresses in colours of sunlight and shades of green and bronze that toned with her hair. There was footwear for all occasions ... and something in a long box that she

61

hardly dared to touch.

With tentative fingers she stroked the honey-brown mink ... surely there was some mistake? Don Juan had not mentioned fur wraps to her, yet one had been sent, a dream-soft cape for the shoulders, with one huge mink button to fasten it and silken straps beneath the fur into which she slipped her arms.

She had put it on as if in a dream and now she found herself in front of the mirror. She stared at her reflection. Pilgrim in a fur wrap. Pilgrim the maid clad like a princess!

A blush ran all over her fair skin. Had she misunderstood Don Juan when he had talked of making her his ward? Manrique Cortez had said that people were talking about her. Had she, in her innocence, led the Marqués to suppose that in return for the lovely clothes she would be compliant to demands other than those of guardianship?

She tore off the wrap, threw it on the bed and went running from the room. She didn't stop running until she reached the door of his study at the top of the sea-tower. She tapped upon it before she lost her nerve. She had to tell him that the clothes were too elaborate; that she wanted only simple things. She had to make things clear to him ... she was a good girl, not one to be bought with mink!

A deep voice invited her in Spanish to enter, and she took a deep breath before turning the handle of the oval-shaped door. She stepped into a circular room, and for a moment she hardly recognized the lean figure who sat behind the heavily carved desk. He wore a silk shirt open at his throat, his hair was disarranged, as if he had been running his fingers through it, and around him hung the strong haze of the dark *cigarros* he was fond of smoking.

It was always disturbing to be in his presence, and upon this occasion Yvain was nervously aware of what she had come to discuss with him.

'So at last you have found your way to my *atalaya*.' He got to his feet and indicated that she sit in a nearby chair upholstered in black velvet. 'It's a word meaning watch-tower, for in the old days men would have been posted up here to keep a lookout for pirate galleons. In fact, a certain scion of the Leon family was once a notorious sea-rover himself.'

Don Juan's smile was a brief flash of white teeth. 'The history of my family has long fascinated me and I am in the process of writing it.' He gestured at the pile of manu-script on his desk, and the leather-bound diaries and notebooks that lay open around him. 'It proves an absorbing task, for the Leons have been soldiers, explorers, sea-rovers and poets.'

Yvain gazed fascinated at his darkly handsome face; in his white silk shirt and with his hair ruffled, he was a magnetizing man. Her heart drummed . . . this was a man who looked as if he might carry in his veins a dash of his pirate ancestor! Made shy by him and by the thought, she pulled her eyes away from him and looked around his study. It was quite austere except for the wall cabinets that held trophies, several rifles, the bric-à-brac of a man who had once been very active. There were Aztec masks, objects found in strange places, and a clump of silver . . . probably the first piece he had ever mined.

She glanced back at him and found him studying her through *cigarro* smoke and narrowed eyes. 'The clothes came . . . from Madrid,' she blurted.

'I hope you found them to your liking,' he drawled.

'Don Juan . . .'

'Yes, Yvain?'

It was his use of her name, the velvety inflexion of his voice, the way he looked at her that made her take panic again. 'Ignazio's have sent a ... a fur wrap, *señor*. You didn't order one—'

'Of course I did.' Deep in his eyes something was flickering. 'A mink shoulder-wrap suitable for a young girl ... don't you like it, *señorita*? Does it not become you?'

'It's beautiful, but I can't accept it!'

'And why not, may I ask?'

'It's too expensive.'

'If the wrap is becoming on you, then I shan't question the cost.'

'I would, *señor*!'

'You, *señorita*?' He lifted his *cigarro* with a deliberate movement of his hand and drew on it. Smoke drifted just as casually from his nostrils. 'Do you expect to pay for the garment as well?'

'Fur wraps are usually paid for twice over.' Her heart was drumming madly, for though his face was so still, his eyes were quietly smouldering. She was gripping the edge of her chair, as if ready to catapult out of it to the door.

It was then that he gave an amused chuckle. 'So, *niña*, you have guessed my wicked intention and won't be bought with furs and flounces, eh? Tut-tut! What a dire disappointment for the black-eyed lord of the castle? What will he do now to entice the innocent maid into his embrace – will he in next week's thrilling chapter find a way to overcome her scruples?'

Yvain stared at him, and then he chuckled again and she blushed scarlet.

'What absurd novels the Señora Sandell must have ordered you to read to her.' He tapped his *cigarro* over a bronze ashtray. 'Child, I give you the new clothes because you need them, and because a young girl should have a few pretty things. I think it has been a long time since anyone gave you presents, so you are suspicious of them. You have no need to be. A fur wrap is necessary when we go to the theatre or to dine with friends of mine. As my ward I expect you to look presentable.'

She swallowed the lump of mortification in her throat. 'I . . . I'm sorry for being so foolish, *señor*.'

'I don't blame you, child. You worked for a foolish woman who no doubt planted in your head the idea that love between adults is a commodity, something to be bought and sold. I am well aware myself that there are people who are imbued with this idea. My grandparents could never understand my father for choosing love in preference to a cold, brilliant alliance with a girl of wealth. To the day of his death they never forgave him.'

Don Juan's eyes dwelt broodingly on the silver he had dug out of the wild land of his youth. 'They called me the son of a witch. They said my mother had cast a gipsy spell over their son . . . they blamed her for his death. Her people were partisans, and she and my father fought in the hills of Spain with them until he was killed.

The dark eyes of the son of Rosalita caught and held Yvain's. They were set deep beneath the black brows, with lines etched outwards to his temples. His temples were smoky-silver, a strange contrast to the vigour of his shoulders, moulded by the silk of his shirt. And then almost with deliberation he rose to his feet and with the aid of his stick he limped to a window of his sea-tower.

'Come and watch the sun as it drowns in the sea,' he said, and he opened the window and the evening air rushed in. Yvain, shy of him because of her foolishness; shy of contact as yet with any man, leaned far forward to look at the sunset. A great flame, burning its way into the water far below, setting light with colour the tips of the silky waves.

'So lovely and cruel,' she breathed.

Her hair took flame as well, and then suddenly she felt a hand upon it. 'Would you escape, Rapunzel?' There was a note of humour in his voice, a questing look in his eyes when she turned to face him.

'My father used to call me that,' she said. 'He used to say that one day I would – *señor*, your castle is very well preserved, yet it must be very old.'

'A mere hundred years, *señorita*.' There was a glimmer in his eyes, as if in retrospect he found it amusing that he should be thought the seducer of a leggy adolescent. 'The old *castillo* was a rambling structure built all over these cliffs and somewhere we have a painting of it, but I consider the present building much more attractive and compact – don't you?'

'I love it.' The words leapt warm from her lips. 'I never ever thought to live in a castle. It's like something out of a fable.'

'And I am the ogre?' he quizzed her, a quirk to his left eyebrow.

'No—'

'Come, why should a young girl not find me rather sinister with my limp and my brooding on the past?'

He turned from her without awaiting her reply and limped back to his desk. 'Tomorrow evening we dine at the Club Hidalgo with Señor Fonesca and his daughter. I should like you to wear one of the new dresses.'

'Yes, *señor*.' She heard the note of dismissal in his voice and walked past him to the door of his tower. There she paused and glanced back at him. 'Thank you for the lovely things, Don Juan. I am grateful – really.'

'They are necessary to your new life.' He spoke crisply and was studying a sheet of manuscript covered in long-hand. 'I shall be working most of this evening, so *vaya con Dios*.'

The beautiful Spanish words travelled with her to her room, where she proceeded to fill the wardrobe and the drawers with her new and exciting possessions. She studied a velvet dress with a full skirt like a bell, and then switched her attention to a chiffon dress with hundreds of fine pleats from shoulders to hem. Never in her life before had she been faced with the problem of choosing a dress in which to dine with a man at a smart nightclub. It was like a dream, yet when she pinched herself the pain was real.

The dresses were real . . . the castle was a fact . . . in the morning she would not awake to the clamour of an alarm clock, to face another day of waiting hand and foot on Ida Sandell. All of that was behind her . . . all of this was part of her new life.

After eating alone, she sat at her bedroom window and watched the stars sparkling over the sea. She breathed the scent of pennyroyal and wondered what Manrique Cortez would think of her in her finery tomorrow evening.

Her heart drummed softly with excitement. Manrique had thought her attractive and as she touched a wondering hand to her hair, she remembered how the young men on the ship had passed her by without a second glance. It had hurt to be a wallflower. It had made her feel so lonely and unwanted to have to watch other girls dancing in the arms of smiling young men, and sometimes she had cried in the silence of the night and longed for someone to say nice things to her.

Manrique had come along and said them, and perhaps

when they met again he might ask her to dance with him.

The following evening she chose to wear the velvet dress. She loved the tawny gold colour of the lustrous material, and most of all the short embroidered jacket that went with the gown. She plaited her hair – washed that morning and the colour of an autumn leaf – and circled the crown of her head with the glossy rope. She then applied face powder, lipstick and a little eye-shadow, for an assortment of cosmetics had been sent with the accessories to her new clothes, and she was thrilled by how adult she looked.

Her eyes shone now they weren't obscured by those awful spectacles, and with a happy laugh she curtsied to her reflection. She was glad she looked nice ... for Manrique ... but now she had to go downstairs and present herself to her guardian.

Her fingers clenched nervously on her velvet embroidered bag as she made her way down to the hall. The turret stairs formed a spiral around her slim young figure and she was almost at the foot of them before she became aware of the tall dark figure framed by an archway leading out from the hall. There was a wall lamp above the archway and it cast its shaded light as if upon a statue ... he didn't move or speak until Yvain's eyes fell startled upon him.

'Oh—' She paused upon the stairs and caught her beaded bag to her heart. 'Good evening, *señor*.'

He held out a hand to her and she went hesitantly towards him. 'You look very grown up,' he said, and for a frightening moment, as he took her hand, she thought he would raise it and kiss it. But no. He pulled her into the light and studied her face. 'You have too much paint on your lips — come!' Gripping her with one hand, and his stick with the other, he made her go with him to the *sala*.

He gestured at a mirror on the wall. 'Wipe off the paint,' he ordered.

She did as she was told, but inwardly she was trembling. Had she expected this man to admire her in the dress he had paid for? What a forlorn hope! He merely wished her to look presentable to his friends.

'Is that better, *señor*?' She turned to face him, and he aroused in her all the awkwardness of youth as he looked her over. Not a flicker of a smile disturbed his countenance as he half-leaned upon his stick and studied her as if she were a painting on a wall instead of a living girl with a heart beating fast beneath the tawny velvet that picked up highlights from the lamps.

His dark eyes dwelt on her bare young neck. 'To put jewels on the young is to gild the lily,' he said, 'but I think you might like to wear this.'

He brought from his pocket a narrow jewel-case and handed it to her. She lifted the lid with fingers that trembled and caught her breath at the strand of twisted gold set here and there with a rose-diamond and tiny leaves of glimmering green stones. 'How unusual,' she breathed. 'Oh, I'd be frightened in case I lost it.'

She was about to shut the case when he put out a hand and took the necklace from its satin bed. 'Come here,' he said, and she didn't dare disobey him, almost holding her breath as she felt the necklace against her skin and the brush of his fingers as he fastened the clasp. 'Turn around, Yvain.'

She did so, and gave a sudden nervous laugh. 'If Mrs. Sandell could see me now!'

'What do you suppose she would say?'

'I think she would be speechless for once, *señor*. You see—'

'Yes, Yvain?'

'I never had a pretty dress before . . . I always looked so awful in beige, and she made me wear spectacles.'

'But your eyes don't look weak to me.' He quirked a black eyebrow and his lean, strong hand took her face and held it as if it were a chalice, or a flower. 'What happened to the spectacles?'

'They were lost . . . in the sea.'

'You must let the unhappy memories be lost as well, *niña*. I promise you will never wear beige while you live in my castle.'

'I'm grateful for your kindness, *señor*.'

'I don't want gratitude, and I am not particularly kind.' His eyes held hers, and then he let her go. 'Come, we have a six-mile drive into Puerto de Leon and I don't wish to keep Raquel and her father waiting for us.'

Yvain preceded him from the room, and from the castle to the limousine. The chauffeur held open the door and she slipped inside with a whisper of velvet. Don Juan followed, somewhat clumsily because of his leg, and his stick fell to the floor of the car. Yvain quickly retrieved it, and she winced as his fingers gripped hers with the stick. He thanked her in a curt voice, and his face had the immobility of a rather cruel mask as the overhead light struck across it.

Yvain shrank away into a corner of the veloured seat as the big car swung out of the gates of the castle, a slim and bewildered young figure in her tawny velvet and borrowed jewels.

She felt as if she would never understand this man who seemed almost human one moment, and then so proud and unapproachable the next. He gave her a home; he

70

fed and clothed her, but he seemed to forbid her to give him anything in return ... least of all sympathy or affection.

She looked through her lashes at his profile and it seemed so hard and flawless that it had to belong to a man of stone.

Yvain had not realized that the Club Hidalgo would be so grand! There were many cars parked in front, and long windows ablazé with light from crystal chandeliers. The air inside was expensively scented, and the orchestra played sophisticated music.

The Marqués de Leon and his ward were greeted with deferential bows and smiles of welcome, and people looked at them as they were led to their table, occupied already by a silver-haired man with a clipped beard, and the beautiful Raquel Fonesca.

'*Que gracia tiene.*' Señor Fonesca was on his feet and Yvain met the shrewd friendliness of his eyes and was at once less nervous. He bowed over her hand as they were introduced and he seemed much nicer, Yvain thought, than his daughter, who was studying the velvet dress and the necklace with speculating eyes.

'Juan,' she said in her warm, throaty voice, 'I would never recognize your ward after the other day. Papa, it was so amusing. This child came from the beach carrying an enormous melon and I thought she was just a school-girl. Tonight you look quite nice ... it is amazing what clothes from the Gran Via can do for one.'

She smiled charmingly at Don Juan as they settled themselves at the table and he turned to consult with the wine waiter. 'I know you are fond of champagne, Raquel, so shall we celebrate with a bottle?'

'That would be delicious, but what are we celebrat-

71

ing?' Raquel's gaze flitted across the table to Yvain. 'Is it your birthday, my dear?'

'No.' Yvain's hands clenched in her lap and her eyes sought Señor Fonesca's. He looked kind, tolerant, and he gave her a feeling of reassurance. 'At least, I do feel reborn, for all this is very new to me.'

Raquel played lazily with her black lace fan, whose pattern of roses matched the colour of her dress. 'I believe you were a companion, were you not?'

'A maid-companion,' Yvain corrected, knowing very well that the other girl knew and had forced her to put it into words.

'No wonder all this should seem like a birthday to you.' Señor Fonesca smiled at her. 'Juan wishes me to teach you Spanish and other subjects, and I think I am going to enjoy being tutor to such a charming young lady.'

Yvain could have hugged him. 'I'm very eager to learn, *señor*. And I warn you I shall be an avid pupil.'

'Oh dear,' Raquel laughed and her eyes flirted with Don Juan over the top of her fan, 'you have a blue-stocking in the family, *amigo*. Father will love cramming her with knowledge, but I think it is much nicer to enjoy life and much more fun to collect sweethearts.'

'Do you see what happens, Juan,' laughed Señor Fonesca, 'when a Spaniard allows his daughter to become emancipated? She immediately reverts to the true Latin type and thinks only of romance.'

'What is nicer to think about than romance?' Raquel coquetted with Don Juan, who seemed to enjoy it in his enigmatic fashion, a quirk to his left eyebrow. 'Of course, if a girl is quite plain, then it is better for her to be clever. I was never very clever.'

Only at insinuation, Yvain thought, and she knew that beside the Spanish girl she looked naïve and awkward, and unused to carrying off with an air a gown from the Gran Via. Her coronet was absurd, she told herself, and her lips felt pallid. Did Don Juan believe that Raquel's lips were naturally like rose petals against her pale golden skin?

The arrival of the waiter with their champagne came as a relief. The cork popped so loudly that it made Yvain jump and Raquel laugh. 'Your first taste of champers?' she asked, using a word that had surely gone out with the cloche hat?

'My very first,' Yvain agreed, watching wide-eyed as it bubbled golden into the wide glasses on their long hollow stems.

'*Salud, amor y tempo,*' smiled Señor Fonesca. 'A true Spanish toast, Señorita Yvain. Love and time, both of which we make the most of.'

After that it was a gay dinner hour, with dishes of a piquant flavour, an easy flow of conversation to which Yvain mainly listened. The orchestra played, couples danced, and she knew that soon in a single spotlight Manrique Cortez would appear and make magic with his voice and his guitar.

The thought made her eyes sparkle, and all at once she became aware that Don Juan was looking directly at her. 'You like the champagne?' he asked.

'It makes one feel – relaxed.' She dared to smile at him, and then her attention was diverted to the floor in front of the orchestra dais, where a lean figure in narrow dark trousers and a ruffled shirt had appeared to a thunder of applause. He bowed, he looked around, and Yvain felt a thrill of excitement as his eyes met hers. He smiled and she felt as if everyone knew that he smiled at her alone.

'*Señoras y señors*, I will sing an old love song of Seville.' He leaned against a pillar and cradled his guitar, and the lights began to dim. 'Imagine a balcony and a girl, and below in the night a young man in love but aware that another man stands between him and his desire.'

Manrique began to play, and it was as if the guitar came alive in his hands; he began to sing and there wasn't a murmur, not a clink of cutlery or wine glass. On the beach the other day Yvain had sensed his magic, and tonight his music mingled with the wine she was unused to and she felt as if she were the girl on the balcony. A girl desired and torn between two men who adored her.

During the applause that followed the song, Doña Raquel remarked that he was very attractive. Yvain was aware of the flick of her eyes, and she shrank inwardly, as if the other girl had the power to spoil her dream.

'He's a fine musician, eh, Juan?' Señor Fonesca leaned forward with a light for the other man's cigar, and his eyes were twinkling. 'But no doubt our two young ladies are more aware of his personality.'

Smoke wreathed about Don Juan's dark eyes, and Yvain felt him looking at her as Manrique began to play some music of Malaga, a wine-treading song which was gay and full of the Latin love of insinuation and rather naughty wit. He moved from the pillar and began to thread his way among the tables, and Yvain's heart was in her throat as he paused beside their table and sang a line of his song just for her . . . then he moved on.

'Well,' chuckled Señor Fonesca, 'at one time only innocent young girls were allowed into the vineyards.'

'No wonder he came to this table.' Raquel's fan was fluttering like the wing of a scolding bird. 'Yvain has been making eyes at him ever since he started to sing.'

For a moment Yvain was speechless, then she looked at the other girl and felt a primitive urge to pull her hair. 'As it happens I know him,' she retorted. 'I met Rique Cortez on the beach the other day and we became friends.'

The chandeliers brightened in that moment and applause for the singer drowned all speech for several minutes. But Raquel's look was eloquent, and Yvain was defiantly aware that her guardian's eyes had narrowed.

'Why did you not invite Señor Cortez to the castle?' he asked, as the applause died away. 'It is customary among Spaniards for a young man to introduce himself formally to a girl's parent or guardian.'

'I'm British,' she replied. 'Such Victorian ways are outmoded in my country.'

At once, deep in his eyes, a flame seemed to burn. 'You will follow our customs while you are a guest in my house. The next time a young man approaches you—'

There he broke off, for as the orchestra began to play dance music, Manrique Cortez approached their table again. Now he was clad formally in a dinner jacket, his face a polite mask as he bowed to the Marqués and his guests.

'Would the Señor Marqués permit that I ask the *señorita Inglesa* to dance?' he inquired. 'We have met, but I take this opportunity to present myself formally to her guardian.'

To Yvain it was like a scene from a play which she watched from a distance, part of the audience instead of one of the stars. She saw Don Juan tap ash from his cigar, while Raquel's fan was held like a broken wing in front of her. 'Señor Cortez, I must congratulate you on your skill as a guitarist,' said Don Juan. 'We were much entertained, and had I known that you were acquainted with my ward I should have asked you to join us in a glass of wine. Perhaps you will do so now?'

'The Señor Marqués is most kind.' Manrique glanced at Yvain and smiled into her eyes. 'It would be more than wine to me if I could dance with the young lady.'

'You wish to dance?' Don Juan was looking directly at Yvain.

'I'd love to,' she said in confusion. 'But I ... I'm not very good at it.'

'Let me teach you, *señorita*.' Manrique drew her to her feet and led her on to the dance floor, and there she was encircled by his arms, while he murmured: 'Hullo again, La Soledad. *Dios*, it was like entering a lion's cage to take you from your stern guardian!'

'I know what you mean.' She laughed shyly as she fell into the rhythm of the music and found Manrique a perfect partner. His arms felt strong around her and his shoulder was at just the right height, shielding her from the gaze of her guardian, and the eyes of Raquel Fonesca.

'You said you were a poor dancer,' Manrique teased her. 'I think you are a mystery girl – come now, with whom have you danced before?'

'With the butler,' she giggled, 'at the servants' Christmas dance when I was a maid. It was considered quite an honour to be asked by Higgins to dance, and when he'd had a few ports there was no holding him.'

She danced for an hour with Manrique. They hardly left the floor, and when they did she found herself on the terrace with him, under the stars, her head and her heart in a whirl. She laughed, softly and breathlessly. 'Oh, I've never had such a good time! Is it midnight yet? Must I dash away in case my finery turns again into a shapeless beige frock?'

'How you intrigue me!' Manrique took her by the chin as if he would kiss her, and at once she took fright and darted down the terrace steps into the garden. He followed, and soon they were lost among the almond trees and the flowering hedges, and she knew herself less nervous here, the shadows and the roses a barrier against Don Juan and his authority over her.

'You are very sensitive, aren't you?' Manrique caught and held her against a tree, and his eyes sparkled down at her like dark stars. 'But I like you the way you are – the girl who is generous with her kisses is a miser with her love.'

'Isn't it a little early in our friendship to start discussing such a subject?' she asked, and though her heart beat fast from the wine and the dancing she wasn't nearly as nervous of Rique as she was of Don Juan, who could so daunt a girl with that black frown of his.

'But no, the Spanish boy and girl talk all the time about love.'

'I'm not Spanish, *señor*,' she said demurely.

'You mean to tell me that you have never discussed *el flechazo* with a young man?'

She shook her head with a smile, for until tonight she had never even danced with a young man; never known the excitement of being alone with someone who was attractive and full of daring remarks. The arrow of love had never flown her way.

'You have been very sheltered,' he said.

'Obscured would be a better word.' Her fingers caressed the bell-like skirt of her velvet dress. 'It still feels so strange to be dressed like this . . . as if I'm masquerading in someone else's clothes.'

'But you are not.' Rique's eyes gleamed down at her in the half-dark. 'The Marqués is a rich man and he has made you his ward. This necklace you wear is set with diamonds and emeralds.'

His fingers touched the stones and she shivered for some odd reason.

'I'm grateful to him,' she said, 'but it's like being –

possessed.'

'How do you mean?' Rique's hands were suddenly gripping her. 'He treats you like a daughter, does he not?'

'Yes—'

'Then why do you talk of being possessed?' Rique's face was close to her and his eyes were no longer smiling. 'We use this word to mean something else. *Te quiero*. I want you! Not as a daughter but as a woman!'

'Don't!' She wrenched away from him. 'I never meant to imply such a thing – Don Juan is my guardian and I meant that he takes it so seriously. He has sent to Spain for a *duenna* for me, and before I make friends with anyone I must present them to him for his approval.'

'Ah, now I understand!' Rique gave a laugh. 'That is how it is with a parent or a guardian. You must expect the Señor Marqués to act in this way, for as his ward you are now a very eligible young lady.'

'What do you mean?' She was perplexed. 'To speak of someone being eligible is to imply marriage and a dowry. I assure you—'

'Now you are annoyed.' Rique touched her cheek as if to feel its embarrassed warmth. '*Carina*, as ward of the Marqués de Leon you will reap all the benefits he can bestow. Surely you know this? A Spaniard takes seriously his responsibilities.'

'But all I want is an education!'

'How charming and innocent you are!' Rique laughed, and caught her in his arms. 'All you need is educating in matters of the heart, so let me be your teacher, let me show you how exciting a kiss can be.'

'No, Rique!' She struggled with him, and then stiffened into stillness as she caught the sound of footsteps limping along the path between the trees. 'Oh – it's him!'

'Yvain?' His sharp ears must have caught her terrified

whisper. 'Where are you?'

She couldn't answer him, and Rique seemed as dumb-struck. There they stood so close together, his arms still around her as Don Juan parted the tresses of the trees with his stick and stared at them. 'We are about to go home,' he said, and his voice was as expressionless as his face. 'Release my ward, if you please, *señor*. She has had quite enough excitement for one evening.'

Rique's arms loosened from around her tense young figure, and she knew she looked as pale and guilty as she felt. Don Juan stood aside for her to pass him, and she heard him say to Rique: 'In future you will remember that Yvain is my ward. Any more of this kissing in the dark and I shall forbid her to see you.'

She turned to protest at this, but he waved her along the path, so tall, dark and grim that she didn't dare to disobey him. She gathered up her velvet skirts and ran ahead of him through the garden. She felt horribly like a child who had been caught doing something naughty, and on the way home in the car she tried to defend her innocence. 'There was no kissing in the dark,' she said, her eyes fixed on the glass panel that separated them from the chauffeur.

'I am quite sure there would have been if I had not come along.'

'Like some Victorian uncle!'

'Is that how it seemed?' A faint smile deepened the lines of irony about his mouth. 'There is a singular inno-cence about you, Yvain, but I know my countrymen and how expert they are when it comes to flirtation. I don't wish you to mistake the ardent talk of a handsome young musician for the deep feelings that have no words. I wish you to get to know Latin people and their ways, and then you will not need the protection of a Victorian uncle.'

Yvain bit her lip. 'I'm sorry to be tiresome, and a burden, *señor*.'

'You add words I did not use, *señorita*.'

'Surely you implied them?'

'You mean by my manner, when I found you in the arms of that young man?'

'I was in his arms on the dance floor ... is there so much difference?'

'My dear child, if you think not, then it looks as though I have other aspects of your education to take in hand.'

She looked at him quickly and again she saw in his dark eyes that disconcerting glimmer of humour. It startled and held her because otherwise his face was unreadable. It was like sunlight held and trapped at the bottom of a pool. A hint of devilry ... a reminder that Juan de Leon had not always been a man with a limp.

'You act the tyrant of iron,' she said, colour in her cheeks, 'just to tease me.'

'Not entirely.' He clasped his hands over the silver top of his stick. 'I meant what I said to Manrique Cortez. He may be a friend to you because you need someone young to talk and dance with ... but I will not tolerate an affair *amore.* Do you understand?'

'Yes, *señor*.' She looked at his profile and the smoky hair at his temple. The blend of vigour and maturity were disturbing, and she wished it were otherwise. She wished this man could be like a father to her. 'I'll try to do as you tell me, but what about my feelings?'

'Your feelings?' He looked deliberately at her, as if it amazed him that she might have any.

'You can't forbid me to fall in love,' she said.

'If you are talking about calf-love, then it is something

we all have to suffer on the way to growing up.'

'I grew up when I was fifteen,' she said quietly, and her fingers hurt themselves against the beads of her evening bag. 'In any case, I don't suppose Rique will want to be friends with me after the way you spoke to him.'

Don Juan looked at her and that left eyebrow of his was at its most satanic. 'Spaniards are not that sensitive. In fact they are most persistent in their search for an ideal.'

'Like Don Quixote?' she half-smiled.

'Exactly.' His dark eyes held hers. 'You have read his adventures?'

'In between bouts of reading love stories to Mrs. Sandell.'

He smiled. 'My library in the sea-tower is stocked with many books in English. They are yours to enjoy.'

She thanked him and thought how subtly he had wooed her away from the realms of romance into the classroom again. She might have Rique for a friend, but the Marqués did not consider that she was ready for love.

What was love? Was it heaven in a tremor, a tightening of arms that would never let go, a brush of lips that slowly, ardently crushed all doubts to silence?

She dreamed a little, as girls will, and had dozed off to sleep when the car came to rest in the courtyard of the castle. Somewhere in her dream a hand touched her hair and a voice murmured her name. 'We are home, Yvain.'

'Home?' she said drowsily, and when she opened her eyes her head was resting on her guardian's shoulder and his dark face was so close that she could have drawn his head down to her and felt his cool, chiselled lips crushing hers.

The thought came and went in a second, so startling

her that she drew hastily away from him.

'Come,' he spoke brusquely. 'You are falling asleep from the champagne and all that dancing with the handsome Manrique. Tomorrow, remember, you start your lessons with Señor Fonesca.'

Back to the classroom, she thought, as she stumbled sleepily out of the car and followed Don Juan's limping figure up the steps to the wide flung door of the *castillo*. They entered and he flung her a brusque, '*Buena noche, niña.*'

CHAPTER FIVE

THE Villa Fonesca was situated above the silky blue ruffling of the water in the bay. Fishing boats rocked beside the sea-mossed walls that towered to hold the cluster of white houses. There were people buying the wares of an open market. There was a chapel with a bell-turret, an impression of sun-hot shadow and bright flowers spilling from baskets and balconies.

Don Juan drove with Yvain to the house, but she learned upon their arrival that it wasn't from a wish to see her safely installed with her tutor. Dona Raquel awaited him, looking as cool and lovely as a flower in a dress of starched white lace and a wide hat with a rose under the brim. She and Don Juan were going across to the mainland for the day. Raquel wished to do some shopping, and the Marqués had business there.

Before they departed, glasses of lemon tea were served on the patio of the villa. It was a place of romantic nooks and twisted old olive trees with a kind of wizardry about them. There was a seat encircling one of the trees and Raquel sat there in her shady hat, graceful and content because for a whole day the lean, dark man in the immaculate white suit would be hers alone.

'You look like a Renoir,' he said to her.

She smiled, and for a moment her eyes dwelt on Yvain in her simple yellow dress with a white butterfly collar. It was sleeveless, showing her slim young arms. The hem was short, revealing her slender legs. Down over one shoulder hung her switch of auburn hair, tied off with a green ribbon.

'Juan, which artist might have painted your ward?' Raquel's lashes fluttered as she looked at him, as if sending some sort of love morse, one of those secret messages that pass between people having a romance.

He leaned in his white suit against a dark tree, while Señor Fonesca sat at his ease in a wicker chair, smoking a cigarette in a bone-coloured holder. 'Dégas.' The *señor* spoke because Don Juan seemed to have no opinion to offer with regard to his ward. 'He alone could have sketched those slender limbs and those great eyes. Always his girls were slightly enchanted, as if like a summer cloud or a pattern on water they might vanish.'

'So, my dear,' Raquel arose with a laugh and a rustle of starched lace, 'you are not *ras de terre* like us? Papa, give the child another slice of almond cake ... we don't want her to float away, do we?'

'Go shopping!' the *señor* laughed. 'Juan, take away this spoiled daughter of mine and leave me with this child whose young mind is not cluttered up with fashion and cocktails and having fun!'

Don Juan smiled, gripped his stick and came across to Yvain. He stood in the attitude she knew so well, half leaning and looking down at her. 'Be a good pupil, *niña*, for I shall ask questions when we meet again.'

She met his eyes and found that he had become again her rather stern guardian. The shoulder she had leaned against was square and unapproachable, the hand that gripped the ebony stick could only have felt gentle in a dream.

'I hope you enjoy your day as much as I expect to, *señor*.' She gave her tutor a quick smile, for her guardian seemed not to want smiles from anyone but Raquel. She alone seemed to hold the key to his enigmatic personality.

'What shall I bring you?' Don Juan asked unexpectedly.

Her eyes widened until she seemed to see no other face but his, dark and distinguished and politely enquiring. She felt Raquel looking on, cool and amused, and yet with her fingers still upon the handle of her woven handbag.

'I . . . I want nothing, Don Juan,' Yvain stammered.

'Not even a box of candies?' he asked, and this time there seemed to be a smile deep in his eyes.

'All right, candies,' she said, and smiled back tentatively at him. 'Not too sugary, please.'

'Caramels?' He quirked an eyebrow and then turned to Señor Fonesca. 'We will be late returning, *amigo*, but I promise not to let your lovely daughter stray too far away from me.'

'Juan, you must not start acting the guardian with me . . . you have no need.' Raquel laughed warmly and took his arm. 'I am not a teenager, you know.'

'I know, Raquel.' He smiled down at her, and to Yvain looking on his expression seemed very worldly in that moment. 'And now we had better be on our way if we are to catch the steamer.'

'*Lo que tu quieras*,' she replied, and Yvain heard Señor Fonesca draw in his breath, as if his daughter had admitted openly to being the Spanish grandee's willing slave.

Don Juan bowed briefly to the *señor*, looked a moment at Yvain, and then he and Raquel departed from the patio, the sound of his stick and her high heels dying away across the hall, followed by the closing of a door.

For a minute or so both Yvain and her tutor seemed content to enjoy the sense of peace that stole over the patio. It was as if conflicting emotions had been at war in the sunshine, but now there was only the natural sound of birds and the trickling of the wall fountain. The villa was a baroque structure with mellow walls, and there was a red oleander tree dripping scent and petals not far from where Yvain sat in a tub chair. Lovely flowers, she thought, but dangerous because of the poison in their sap.

'So, my child, you have a longing to learn things.' The *señor* made a steeple of his fingers and studied Yvain with a look of shrewd and friendly interest. 'Was it your own idea, or that of Don Juan? He is a young man of strong will, and it is unusual for a pretty girl to wish to study with a crusty professor the philosophy of art and literature. Most young girls have romance on their minds.'

She cupped an oleander flower and smiled shyly. 'I never had a real education, *señor*, and it's like a miracle that Don Juan should bring me to you to be tutored. I want to learn, to absorb, to grow up through learning. One stays immature without knowledge.'

'Ah.' A glint came into the *señor*'s eyes. 'It might be thought unusual for a bachelor to have a ward, but it is the ward who is unusual. Juan is not a sentimental man. Had you been the foolish sort, I am sure he would have packed you off home with some money and a polite bow. He tells me you have no family?'

'Not any more, *señor*.'

'That is sad for you, and lonely. Everyone should have someone, which is one of the clichés I don't mind using. Perhaps you look upon Juan as a sort of uncle?'

'No—' She broke into a smile that turned to a laugh. 'I can't really imagine myself calling him Tio Juan. He's much too aloof and important ... he's the lion of this island.'

'And you regard yourself as a caprice of his?'

'Yes.'

'Do you know, my child, that there is cruelty and lone-liness in the Spanish male?'

'I know it now.'

'Juan has given you cause already to know it?' Señor Fonesca leaned forward, his eyes intent upon her face. 'In what connection?'

'He objects a little to my friendship with Manrique Cortez. I . . . I suppose he considers me too immature to know how to handle a sophisticated person like Rique.'

'You enjoy the company of this young man, eh?'

'Not having had many friends, *señor*, it's always nice to find one. Rique's gay and good-looking and—'

'You feel flattered.' The *señor* smiled. 'Which is only natural. Having a daughter of my own, I know how much it means to a girl to be thought appealing.'

'Doña Raquel is beautiful.' Yvain spoke sincerely, though she had doubts about the beauty of the other girl's nature. 'She must always have been admired.'

'From a child,' her father admitted, not without a gleam of pride in his eyes. 'She resembles her mother, but Anna was gentle and kind and our few years together were very happy ones. My Raquel is a bit of a handful, and I am inclined to pity in advance the man whom she decides to marry.'

Yvain was absently shredding the petals of a flower, and she had a vivid mental picture of Raquel's jewelled hand tucked into the crook of a white-clad arm. Raquel Fonesca had decided that it would be to her advantage, and also exciting, to become the bride of the Marqués de Leon. What, then, would happen to Don Juan's ward?

'Of what are you thinking, my child, with your eyes all misted with mystery?'

Yvain looked at her tutor and summoned a smile. 'Life,

when you come to think about it, is a very mysterious thing. Is it true that our path is plotted even before we are born?'

'*El destino?*' The *señor* looked thoughtful. 'I am inclined to think that each of us has a crossroads in his life – ah, you open wide the brown-gold eyes! Have I said something significant, *señorita?*'

'Yes – it's strange.' The petals dropped from her hand as she studied her palm, in which a fairground gipsy had seen a crossroads. She told her tutor of that palm reading and waited for him to smile, but he didn't.

'The true Romany has the gift of clairvoyance,' he said. 'Your guardian's mother was a Spanish gipsy, and I sometimes wonder if she knew in advance that her marriage to Juan's father would end in tragedy. The old Marqués de Leon would not accept the girl, and when tragedy struck and she became a widow she fled with her baby son to South America. Juan grew to manhood there, and being strong-willed and ambitious he made good without the help of his father's family. It was out in Lima . . .'

Señor Fonesca broke off and studied Yvain's intent young face. 'You have the capacity to listen quietly to a man . . . has Juan ever unmasked to you or revealed a little of his pain?'

'His pain?' she echoed, remembering moments when he seemed lost in a dark sea of brooding, the lines etched deep beside his mouth. Times when his frown frightened her and she kept out of his way.

'That leg of his still troubles him. In the beginning the doctors out in Lima wished to amputate, but he wasn't having that and he travelled all the way to England, where he placed himself in the care of a bone surgeon who set about rebuilding the leg, a protracted and agonizing series of operations, months of being encased to his hip in a plaster cast, setbacks, torment, his nerves drawn taut by the onslaughts of pain. It was a miracle that he kept the leg at all, which was shattered and crushed when the horse he was riding broke a hoof bone. Juan liked to gallop at a fast pace across the wild country and his mount was bounding up a hillside when the accident happened. Juan was thrown, the horse rolled upon him and his left leg was crushed.'

Yvain caught her breath and pictured vividly what it must have been like, the headlong fall of the horse, the plunging, lashing brute strength, pinning the Marqués by his left leg.

'He must have been all alone,' she said in a stricken voice, 'out there in the wilds.'

'For some hours, until some *vaqueros* came along and found him, delirious in the hot sun, the horse dead beside him from the bullet he had fired to put the animal out of its misery. He once told me that only the thought of the gun in his belt kept him sane during those waiting hours. He knew he could go the way of the horse if his agony became too great to bear.'

'Only someone with a will of iron could have borne such a nightmare,' Yvain whispered. 'The pain, the hot sun, the awareness that he was alone and helpless.'

'Don Juan is both a Spaniard and a gipsy, my child, of the kind who set out long ago to conquer new worlds and who suffered tortures and made others suffer. Because of that strength born in him, that control of emotions and nerves, he survived the accident, the exposure in the sun, the long months of slow healing, and he returned to Spain, to dwell alone in the haunted splendour of the *castillo*. Haunted for him because of the unhappiness his mother had known there.'

'I've seen her portrait,' Yvain said softly. 'It would be

hard for him to forgive those who had hurt her. How could they, when she was like a lovely dark rose?'

'Yes, Rosalita.' The *señor*'s gaze dwelt sombrely on the roses that grew against a wall of the patio. 'I met her on a brief visit to the island. In those days I had a professorship at a college in Madrid and I had not yet made my home on the Isla del Leon. I met Rosalita only a short while before she and Juan's father left the island never to return. She had a glow about her, a kind of witchery. The Marquesa, Juan's grandmother, was a forbidding and unbending woman. She had chosen a girl for her son to marry, but he chose to make a gipsy dancer his wife . . . not only his wife but the future Marquesa . . . and for that his family never forgave him.'

'How snobbish!' Yvain exclaimed. 'To think class and wealth more important than love!'

Señor Fonesca gave the soft, slightly cynical laugh of middle-age. 'The passions of youth, my child, have little value in the eyes of people who have never known them. In Juan's family it was natural for money to marry money; for prestige to be wedded to prestige. His father broke a long-established rule, and I sometimes wonder . . .'

'Yes, *señor*?'

'About Juan, the son of a rebellious noble and a lovely gipsy witch. If it had not been for his accident, which quietened the restless spirit in him, I don't think he would have assumed his title or his position here. Juan de Leon is two men. Catch him unaware and you will see the caged lion in his eyes. At other times the ironic humour of the Spaniard who accepts what has to be. *El destino*.'

It was warm on the patio, yet Yvain gave a cold little shiver. Destiny could be cruel to some people, and she hoped that Don Juan was meant to find happiness to make up for the pain he had suffered. It had put lines in his face, silver in his hair, and deprived him of the ability to leap into the saddle of a spirited horse, to play tennis, to take a girl in his arms so they might enjoy together the fun and rhythm of a dance.

'How old is Don Juan?' she found herself asking.

'He's thirty-two, *niña*.'

'I thought him much older! Why, he treats me like an infant!'

Her tutor laughed. 'To Juan I expect you seem very young and innocent. I believe he lived up to his name out in Lima, a city of lively and exotic ladies.'

'Don Juan,' she murmured. 'The great lover whose heart was never touched.'

'The legend is that he did fall in love – just once.'

'Really?' Her eyes widened and filled again with the image of Raquel clasping his arm with jewelled fingers. He had glanced down at the Spanish girl with worldly eyes, admiring her beauty and wit, and perhaps ready at last to let his heart be captured.

'It is now time we began our lessons.' Señor Fonesca rose to his feet. 'The *sala* is cool and there are books and objects of art for you to study.'

The *sala* – a room Yvain was to become very familiar with – was set out with furniture of the Isabella period. Dark, richly carved, so that the *señor's* art collection was more graceful and colourful by comparison.

Yvain noticed at once some delightful figures of children in terracotta and she was allowed to handle them carefully.

'You must love objects of art with a pang of the heart,' she was told.

'These are charming,' she said, but as she stroked the figures she felt nothing but an admiring interest. She looked at the paintings on the panelled walls, and saw the eyes of real people instead of the painted eyes. She felt shaken. Inanimate things, no matter how beautiful, could not give her a heart pang. Only people could do that. Only anger or compassion or joy.

'Charming,' she said again, and felt her tutor's eyes dwell shrewdly upon her.

'We will begin with the story of Titian.' The *señor* took a large book from the shelves. 'I think you will be more in sympathy with his personality to begin with . . . it is later on that you will be ready for the master.'

Her eyes questioned, large and honey-coloured.

'Leonardo da Vinci,' the *señor* smiled, but it seemed to Yvain that he meant and implied something quite different.

CHAPTER SIX

TODAY was Sunday . . . no lessons, and a note from Manrique Cortez to ask her to go for a drive around the island.

The letter was handed to her at the breakfast table, so she was obliged to ask Don Juan if it would be all right for her to go. He glanced up slowly from his own mail. 'I have said that I have no objection to the young man . . . as a friend, Yvain. Of course you may go driving with him.'

'Thank you.'

'It would seem, in any case, that we must dispense with the idea of a *duenna* for you. I have received an answer from Dona Augusta with regard to my invitation to her. She has to decline on the grounds that she has started a small business and cannot possibly leave it to undertake a service that would not be permanent.' His smile was a mere flicker of the lips. 'Do you think you can bear to remain at the *castillo* without a chaperone?'

'Why should I need one?' she asked.

'Why indeed?' He quirked an eyebrow. 'But I seem to recall that you had doubts about my intentions when the new clothes arrived from Madrid.'

'I know you better now, Don Juan.'

'Do you really?' He reached for the coffee pot and re-filled his cup. 'You have now arrived at the conclusion that I am not like my namesake, eh?'

'He was a heartless philanderer.'

'And what am I?'

She gave a rather confused laugh. 'You are a man of sophistication, and it must have amused you terribly that

I was gauche enough to misunderstand your kindness—'

'Why do you insist on calling me kind, a most avuncular thing to be?' He drank his coffee black. 'My actions are rarely motivated by sentiment. I am a practical man, like most Spaniards, and I don't like to see youth and intelligence wasted, least of all on a vulgar woman. I am pleased by the progress you are making with Señor Fonesca. He tells me that you have a natural aptitude for our language. Come, say something in Spanish!'

'I couldn't!'

'Don't be coy with me!' The lift of his eyebrow was mocking. 'Try to behave as if I were Manrique Cortez.'

'That's impossible!'

'Why, because he's of your generation and I am old enough to be your uncle?'

'I . . . I don't think of you as an uncle,' she protested.

'But you are afraid I shall pounce, so you refuse to speak a few words of Spanish to me.'

'You . . . make me feel shy.'

'Shall I turn my back?' he mocked. 'Really, Yvain, you say I am kind, but all the time you think me stern. Yes, Luis?' He glanced at the hovering manservant.

'Señor Cortez has called for the young lady, señor. He waits in his car.'

'Gracias, Luis.' Don Juan looked at Yvain. 'No doubt you are impatient to join your admirer, so we will continue our discussion another time. Yvain, remember what I said to you. You are my ward and I don't wish people to get the idea that young Cortez is courting you.'

'I shall be very circumspect, señor.' She was so looking forward to the drive that her eyes were sparkling as she jumped up from the table. 'I don't know what time I shall be home . . .'

'That is hardly a concern of mine.' Her guardian spoke

94

coolly. 'I am going out myself.'

'Oh – I hope you enjoy yourself, *señor*.'

'I am sure you will enjoy yourself, Yvain.' He gave her a brief bow. 'Run away, child. Don't keep the young man waiting.'

'No – good-bye.'

'*Hasta la vista, niña.*' He said it rather pointedly, as if reminding her that he wished her to speak Spanish now and then.

She sped away from his daunting presence, across the hall to where Luis held open the front door. As she passed the manservant she felt the flick of his eyes, not quite so unfriendly as they had been, as if the presence of a young person in the house was a novelty. 'You have a fine day, *señorita*,' he murmured.

'Yes, Luis.' She smiled at him. 'In England when we have such sunshine, the day usually ends with rain.'

Luis glanced at the brilliant sky. 'I don't think the *señorita* need worry.'

'There you are, Yvain!' Manrique stood at the bottom of the steps, his smile a flash of white against his dark olive skin. She ran down to him, registering his attraction in a cream jacket, black silk sweater, dark trousers and sandals. He caught hold of her hands and swept his eyes over her. She wore a white dress encircled by a bronze-coloured belt, and her shoes were of bronze. The sun found little lights in her eyes and in her switch of auburn hair.

'Each time I see you,' he smiled, 'you seem a little more grown up. You are rather like a flower which was all closed up in the shade, now our sunshine is revealing an unexpected beauty.'

'Don't be silly,' she gasped. 'I'm not even pretty!'

'What has being pretty to do with beauty?' He handed

her into his car, a sleek cream roadster with caramel-coloured upholstery. All the fittings gleamed in the sunlight, so Yvain guessed it was a brand new car. The top was open, but linen covers prevented the leather from getting too warm.

'All Latin men are flatterers,' she scoffed.

'Even Don Juan?' Rique gave her a rakish look as he took the driving-seat beside her.

'My guardian is a man of responsibility—'

'He's a Spaniard and he has a quick pair of eyes.' Rique started the car and they moved towards the open gates and the sun-hot road. The sea far below was a dazzling silver-blue, and the air held a magic quality. 'He's still quite a young man . . . to have you for a ward.'

'I hope you don't think—'

'Of course I don't.' He gave a laugh. 'It is perfectly obvious to me that no man has yet made love to you.'

'Can't you talk about anything but love?'

'There is no other subject quite so fascinating. It is part of the mystery of life, the most exciting part of being alive.'

'You must often have been in love, Rique, to speak with such authority.'

'What Latin is not a lover, with words and music if not with deeds? Can it be, *chica,* that you quail at the thought of love?'

'I think you confuse love with flirtation.'

'I hope I am allowed to flirt with you?'

'It hardly comes under the heading of friendship.'

'If your guardian expects me to treat you as if you are a schoolgirl, then he might as well lock you in his tower. Shall I turn the car around and take you home to him?'

'No – he's going out.'

'With the exotic Raquel?'

'I expect so.'

'The island abounds with the rumour that he intends to marry her. Do you think he will?'

'He would hardly confide in me.'

'I don't think you will like it much if he marries her.'

'Why should I mind?' She gave Rique a startled look.

'If Raquel should become mistress of the castle, she might resent the presence there of her husband's attractive young ward.'

'Don Juan has not become my guardian for always. He is kind enough to want to help me and I am staying at the castle while Señor Fonesca teaches me some of the things that will help me to start a career.'

'Are you serious?' Rique slowed the car a little as they rounded a curve of the road and this enabled him to take a look at her. Her hair was whipped by the wind and she looked young and appealing, and unaware of the fact.

'It will be more enjoyable than being a maid,' she said

'I can think of something even more enjoyable . . . you could get married yourself.'

'I should want to fall in love before I took that step.'

'But you are afraid of love,' he teased her.

'I'm no more afraid than any other girl, but I am cautious. Oh, Rique, look at the sea! It looks so beautiful that I can hardly believe it terrified me.'

They sped along through the sunshine, and Yvain drank in everything with eager eyes, storing up the things of today so that she might have them to remember when the time came for her to leave the island. They passed almond orchards and olive terraces, and upon a hill stood a windmill straight out of the pages of *Don Quixote*, and the mountains of Spain appeared violet in the distance.

'Is the island like Spain?' she asked.

'Very much so. It's as if someone long ago stole a piece

of Andalusia and set it down in the ocean. I am from the south and I could grow very fond of living here.'

'You are much too cosmopolitan,' she smiled. 'Your music and your singing will take you all over the world, and you know it.'

'Perhaps I do,' he admitted.

'I wonder,' she said, 'if we shall both remember this drive in the sunshine? This moment as we pass a white-walled house smothered in purple flowers? This next moment when we see a lone figure on the beach collecting seaweed and piling it into a donkey-cart? I can smell the seaweed and the flowers, and maybe there will come a time when I shall smell them again and just by closing my eyes I shall remember.' She looked at Rique, studying his Latin profile. 'Will you remember?'

'Memories are too nebulous,' he said. 'I want to hold what lives and breathes.'

'That's because you are a man. I think men remember only the things that hurt them.' She thought of Don Juan, who would never have returned to take his title, or to live in the castle of his grandparents, if he had not suffered that fearful accident. Even yet, her tutor had said, there were times when he was in pain.

'Of what are you thinking?' Rique had brought the car to a standstill and the sound of the sea filled the air, and the hot sun drew the tang of it. She took deep breaths of the sea air and felt safe sitting here; she could not feel the powerful embrace that in the dark had sought to overwhelm her.

Rique took hold of her hand, his thumb against the fragile bones of her wrist. 'For a moment just then, Yvain, you had the unseeing look of someone in a dream. Who wanders in and out of your daydreams?'

'Oh – all sorts of people.' She gave a laugh, but her

pulse jerked and she wondered if he felt it.

'You are a disturbing little thing, Yvain. Lots of girls are conscious flirts. They enjoy making eyes at a man, but you don't even know how to. Your life until now must have been a very sheltered one.'

'It was restricted, which is a different thing. A girl without parents can't be sheltered, Rique, so don't treat me as if I were an infant.'

'I should like to treat you like a sweetheart.' His good-looking face came close to hers, forcing her to retreat along the cushioned seat.

'Rique—'

'Taboos have been imposed, and they tempt a man.'

'Please don't spoil our day together.'

'I am doing my best to improve it. Take a look around you, we are quite alone but for the seaweed-gatherer. Your guardian is nowhere in sight, and is probably courting Doña Raquel with all the aloof gallantry of a true *hidalgo*.'

'Can't you be more aloof?' she begged, for now his left hand had closed upon her waist, and his right hand was touching her auburn hair. She didn't fight with him, for curiously enough his touch did not arouse that tense, crackly feeling, as if his fingertips held an electrical current. It was only when her guardian touched her that she felt this . . . his fingers against her nape as he fastened the necklace; his fingers upon her hair as she leaned from the window of his tower and he called her Rapunzel.

'I thought we were going to have lunch at a *finca*,' she said to Rique.

'In a while.' He drew her suddenly close to him and pressed his lips against the side of her neck. 'You have the untouched skin of a *chica*. Soft, like a petal, with such a clean smell. I must kiss you!'

He did so, but found her lips unresponsive. He studied her face, and she saw a look of perplexity in his eyes.

'Are English girls as cold as snow?' he asked.

'Yes, when they're kissed against their will,' she replied.

'I see.' He withdrew his arms from around her. 'I take it that you find me unattractive?'

'No, Rique. I just want to get to know you better. I want to be friends—'

'Friends – a man and a girl?' He laughed scornfully. 'You would not be here in my car if you were a girl I did not wish to kiss.'

'Is that all you care about, the wrapping and not the contents?' She fumbled with the door of the car, found the release handle and scrambled out with a flash of slim young legs and bronze-coloured shoes. 'Thank you for the drive—'

'Yvain, don't be a little idiot!'

'Little idiots don't mind necking in cars!' she flung at him, and seeing that the shore sloped to the beach she tugged off her shoes and ran down the slope to the sands. She heard Rique give chase and saw with dismay that the seaweed gatherer and the donkey-cart had left and she was alone on the beach with an angry young man in pursuit of her.

'Yvain . . . you are behaving like a child!'

Perhaps she was, but all at once she disliked Rique and wanted him not to touch her any more. She quickened her pace, speeding lightly along the sands and unhampered by the drag of her shoes. She saw a wooden breakwater and scrambled over it, and at once she came in sight of a small pier with a pathway cut into the rocky shore and leading to the steps of the pier. A few moments more and she was mounting the steps, out of breath and relieved to see quite a few people on the pier taking the sun.

She put on her shoes and joined the strollers. She saw Rique gazing up at her from the beach, and then he turned his back on her and strode off to where he had left his car. She wasn't sorry to see him go, and with a smile she joined a young boy who had a rod and a line and was fishing with great seriousness.

'Have you caught anything?' she asked in her faltering Spanish.

'Soon I will catch a fish of great enormity,' he assured her.

She didn't make the mistake of laughing, and in about half an hour, to the amazement and delight of both of them, he caught a sizeable fish and invited her to share it, grilled over a driftwood fire on the beach.

Yvain had set out for the day and it had promised to be carefree, and despite her tiff with Rique she enjoyed every moment of the next few hours. Her young boyfriend's name was Fernando, and he had a loaf of Spanish bread in his knapsack, a bag of tomatoes, and the utensils for cleaning and eating a fish.

They collected their driftwood and made their fire, and the fish when grilled was smoky and delicious, eaten with chunks of crusty bread and huge tomatoes. They lazed in the sun while their meal settled, and then they played volleyball.

It was all such unexpected fun that Yvain didn't realize, until Fernando said it was time for him to go home, that she was miles from the *castillo*. Her young friend pointed out the direction she should take. 'It is much of a walk, *señorita*.'

She bit her lip. 'The fish was splendid. Thank you for letting me share it, Fernando.'

'It gave me pleasure, *señorita*.' He gave her an old-fashioned look, however, for her hair was a tangled cloud about her neck and shoulders and the hem of her dress was soaked with seawater, for several times she had run into the water after the ball. 'You live in earnest at the *castillo* of the Señor Marqués?' he asked.

'Very much in earnest,' she smiled, holding out a hand to him. '*Adios*, Fernando. I hope we meet again some time.'

He didn't shake her hand as she expected him to, but with Latin gallantry he bent over it and kissed it. '*Hasta la vista, señorita*.'

Yvain felt lonely as the sturdy young figure marched out of sight. Soon the sun would be setting and her shoes were of the flimsy type that were not meant for hiking in. However, standing here feeling sorry for herself would not get her home, and she began to hasten along in the late afternoon sunshine, following the sea road as Fernando had instructed, and noticing absently that the mountains of Spain were swathed in mist but for their peaks. Small wreaths of mist were caught in the rays of saffron sunlight that shafted over the water.

The scene was mysteriously beautiful, a little sinister, but half an hour passed before Yvain halted for a rest and noticed that the sun was veiled by mist as it begun to set. She gazed at the sea and a shiver of coldness ran over her. Soon it would be dark and it looked as if the sea mist was creeping inland. She began to hurry . . . and then all at once gave a little yelp as her foot turned and the heel of her right shoe came off. She rubbed the pain from her ankle and gazed ruefully at her heelless shoe.

'This is not your day,' she muttered to herself, and the misty darkness crept around her as she hobbled along, and she watched hopefully for the castle turrets to loom out of the darkness.

Beads of moisture began to form on Yvain's hair and she heard – drifting over from the Spanish coast – the eerie sound of fog-horns on the ships making for harbour. She hobbled a little faster, and the mist followed. She felt apprehensive but not too scared. Once or twice she had been lost on the misty moors of Combe St. Blaize, but being a country girl she had not panicked. That was the thing to avoid, for once panic led you astray you could be lost for hours.

She took her bearings and guessed that within a very short time she would be up to her eyes in a damp fog and she would have to rely on her instincts and her nerves to get her home. She knew there were cottages hereabouts, but they were tucked into the hillside hollows and she didn't dare to leave the side of the road in case she couldn't find it again.

She remembered saying to Luis that morning that a brilliantly fine day in England often led to a storm. She hadn't dreamed that the sunshine of this island could turn suddenly to the menace of a thick sea fog, but here she was, caught in it and feeling almost as helpless as a fly trapped in a jar of honey. She felt lonely and cold and was wishing she had a jacket to put on when a sound behind her made her turn quickly to look.

For the first time in over an hour the lights of a car were heading towards her, stabbing the misty darkness like a pair of beacons. Her heart bounded. At all costs she must stop the car and beg a lift . . . she must!

She ran out headlong into the road, and as her white dress was illuminated by the headlights the driver had to swerve to avoid hitting her. The car brakes were applied jarringly, but a second too late . . . with a grinding of metal and a sound of breaking glass the car crashed into a tree and a dull silence followed.

Anxious and alarmed, Yvain ran across to the car and started to fumble with the door. Someone thrust it open from the inside, and despite the swirling mist and the odd slanting light of the remaining headlamp she recognized the lean figure, the grim face and black hair, the dark and burning gaze that in a second swept away her chills and sent a wave of heat all over her.

In the mist and that oddly angled light they stared at each other.

'Are you . . . all right?' Yvain gasped.

'No thanks to you,' he replied cuttingly. 'I take it you are lost in the fog?'

'Yes, *señor*.' She was half tearful with the shock and relief of seeing him, unhurt at the wheel of the car. The bonnet was badly buckled and when he tried the engine there was a knocking sound but no response. She had known that he drove alone sometimes, in a car so constructed that he had sufficient room in which to stretch his leg.

As Yvain thought of his leg and the hurt it had already suffered she felt sick and had to catch at the door handle.

'I hope your leg wasn't jarred?' she said faintly.

'Everything is all right except for my car and my temper. Why could you not have stood at the roadside and waved me to a halt? My headlamps would have spotted you in that white dress.'

'I . . . I didn't think of anything but getting a lift. I'm sorry about your car . . . is there some damage to the engine?'

He tried once again to get a response from it, but it merely knocked a hole in the silence of the mist-shrouded night. 'There would appear to be damage to the engine,' he said dryly. His glance swept over her, and then he moved along the front seat, put out a hand and pulled her inside with him. 'Close the door and shut out the fog,' he said.

She did so, while he opened a compartment beneath the dashboard and took from it a flask that glinted dully. 'Take a drink of this brandy.' He unscrewed the top and handed her the flask. 'You are shivering, Yvain.'

She clasped her hands about the flask and took small swigs of the warming *coñac*.

His eyes glinted in the glow of the dashboard, half with concern, half with exasperation. 'You females . . . because the sun shines you go out without a coat, careless of the weather and its fickleness. You have had sufficient *coñac*?'

'Mmm, yes.' She returned the flask to him. 'I feel a lot less shivery.'

'There is a laprobe on the back seat, if you will reach over for it.'

She knelt on the front seat so she could reach for the robe. Her fingers came in contact with something soft and velvety, and she gave a little gasp of pleasure when she found that the laprobe was made of some kind of smooth fur.

'Wrap yourself in it,' Don Juan ordered. 'Your dress has no sleeves and barely any skirt.'

She felt her cheeks tingle at the way he looked at her, and her heart quickened when he leaned forward and drew the fur around her, his fingers warm against her throat. 'I saw Cortez at the Hidalgo this afternoon. I asked him where you were, and he said you had returned to the *castillo*. What happened, Yvain? Did you have a quarrel with him?'

'We had a difference of opinion,' she admitted, held by his hands and his eyes.

'What about?'

'Oh, nothing very important. You know how arguments develop from pinpricks.'

'The young man seemed to me to be in a smouldering mood. Did he try to ... make love to you?'

'No ...'

'The truth, Yvain, if you please.'

'He wanted to kiss me ... I wasn't in the mood.' She tried to make light of the matter by giving a laugh. 'Not before lunch.'

'I take it you have been wandering about all day ... without any lunch!'

'I had a delicious lunch,' she protested. 'I made friends with a boy called Fernando. He was fishing from a pier and he shared his catch with me. We cooked the fish over a driftwood fire and had bread and tomatoes with it.'

'Fernando, eh? I hope he proved less ardent than your other *caballero*?'

Now she laughed in earnest. 'He was most gallant and very charming,' she smiled. 'He kissed my hand when we parted.'

'It would have been rather more gallant of the young man to see you arrived home safely.'

Don Juan looked so stern that she couldn't stop laughing. He took her by the shoulders and shook her. 'Why are you laughing at me?' he demanded. 'What is so amusing?'

'Only that my young man of the beach was eleven years old, *señor*.'

'You little devil,' the grip of his hands tightened, 'so you would tease me, eh?'

She looked at him and her laughter died away as she became aware of the intimacy of being alone with him, stranded in the mist, shut in a car with the man who out in Lima had been as wicked and charming as his namesake. That current of awareness slowly generated into a force that half frightened her. She dragged her gaze from his and turned to look out of the window.

'We might be the only two people in all the world,' she said. 'Will the mist clear, do you think, *señor*?'

'Not until dawn.'

The words were like a magnet, drawing her gaze back to him. 'Do you mean we shall have to stay here ... all night?'

'Do you find the prospect daunting?' His eyes held a wicked twinkle by the glow of the dashboard. 'We will wait a while to see if another car comes along to give us a lift, if not then we shall have to seek a proper shelter for the night. The windscreen has lost some glass, do you see? The fog is seeping in.'

It came like little puffs of cold breath and Yvain drew the fur laprobe around her and cuddled down into it. Don Juan opened a thin gold cigarette-case and held it out to her. 'Come, take a cigarette. It will steady your nerves for the possible ordeal of spending the night alone with me.'

'Your turn to tease me, Don Juan.' She accepted a cigarette, a habit she didn't often indulge but one she had acquired during the years with Ida Sandell. A smoke behind the pantry door had sometimes helped to calm her nerves after being bowled out by madam for not pressing a skirt just right, or for tugging her carroty hair with the setting comb.

She leant forward to the flame proffered by her guardian, and the strangeness of these past few weeks seemed to intensify into a single searing moment. All that had happened before the night of the shipwreck had taken on the formless shape of something dreamed. She was alive in this moment as never before. The tang of her cigarette mingling with his, the windscreen with its shattered glass, the vivid dark eyes seen through the smoke . . . these were painfully real to her.

'Do you like small boys?' he asked, unexpectedly.

'Yes,' she smiled. 'Fernando was fun to be with, and that's how come I was late starting for home.'

'Do you think of the castle as your home?'

'In a way.' She met his eyes through the smoke. 'I hope you don't mind?'

'Not at all. I think the *castillo* has waited a long time for someone young to come along and dispel the shadows. When the time comes—'

'For me to go?' she broke in.

He didn't reply for several seconds, his eyes unreadable behind their veil of smoke. 'Yes, it will seem strange for a while, and now we must think about tonight. It will grow gradually colder in here, for that blow to the engine appears to have put the car heater out of order. I could block up the windscreen with something, but neither of us would rest very comfortably.'

'Your leg is aching, *señor*?'

'A little,' he admitted. 'Sometimes I wish I had let the sawbones have their way, but I am obstinate and I dislike what is artificial.'

'Señor Fonesca told me of your accident,' she said, half afraid of showing her sympathy. 'It must have been terrible for you.'

'No more than for a soldier in battle, but I refused to lose my leg, and so whatever aches and pains I now have to tolerate are due entirely to my own self-will.' His smile was a narrow gleam of white teeth. 'Spaniards are not easy on themselves, or on other people, *niña mia*. Study our paintings, read our books, remember our *conquista-dores*.'

'There is a feeling of steel and flame and calvary,' she murmured. 'One feels it here on the island, and sees it in the faces of the people. They are like the faces in portraits by Diaz, like the eyes El Greco painted.'

'El Greco understood Spain and its people, though he was a Greek. Perhaps it takes someone from a foreign land to know us better than we know ourselves, eh?'

She met his eyes and saw combined in his face all the elements that went to make Spain so warm and cruel and fascinating a country. Its people were fashioned out of the rocks, the hot sunshine, and the deep shadows. They combined aloofness with passion, and made one very aware of life and its fundamentals.

'Señor Fonesca is teaching me all about Spain,' she smiled.

'And do you like what you are learning?'

'I am fascinated, *señor*.'

'By the people or the history or the topography?'

'By everything. The people are their history and their land.'

He looked at her as he stubbed out his cigarette. 'What a mixture of wisdom and folly I have in my ward.'

'It's being young, *señor*.'

'Of course.' He leaned forward and studied her wide, fey eyes, her slimness half lost in the laprobe of dark shining fur. 'You are very young in some ways, and yet I can see why Cortez was smouldering when I spoke to him. What did you do – slap his face?'

'No.' She smiled nervously. 'I hopped out of his car and ran away from him.'

'Did he give chase?'

'Yes, until I reached the pier. There were people there, and so I was safe.'

'From his unwelcome attentions?'

'Yes.' Her fingers gripped the laprobe. 'Men seem to think that being alone with a girl gives them the right to be . . . amorous.'

'We are alone, *niña*.' There was a tiny wicked smile at the edge of Don Juan's mouth. 'Are you not afraid of my amorous instincts?'

'You are my guardian,' she said.

'I don't make you want to run away from me?'

She gazed at him, lost for words and aware of his lean strength and darkness with her every nerve. The lines beside his mouth were softened by the shadows and the silver in his hair could not be seen. For a dizzying moment it was as if she found herself alone with the young and daring Don Juan, who had liked fast horses, who had mined for silver in the wilds, and enjoyed the company of exotic women.

All through her young and untried being she was more uncertain of Don Juan than she could ever be of other men.

To her relief he turned his attention to the glove compartment from which he took a hand torch. He flicked on the bright beam. 'I suggest that we go and look for a night's lodging at one of the cottages just off this road. Keep that laprobe cloaked around you.'

They emerged from the car on to the mist shrouded road and Yvain gazed around nervously. All sounds were muted. The trees loomed like ghosts in the creeping greyness. 'Wouldn't it be wise to stay in the car, *señor*?'

'No.' He spoke firmly. 'You would be risking a chill, and I have this uncomfortable limb of mine. Come, stay close to me and I promise that soon you will be sitting beside a warm fire and drinking hot coffee.'

The beam of his torch pierced the mist and in a while they found themselves on a footworn path that had to lead to a habitation of some sort. Yvain did as she was told and kept close to her guardian, who was limping more heavily than usual. It was the dampness, seeping into the bones of the leg that had been rebuilt with such torture and slowness, and she wanted to tuck her fingers into the crook of his arm — as Raquel had done so intimately — and impart a little comfort. It always seemed to hurt more if you kept pain to yourself.

'Ah!' He came to a sudden standstill and Yvain's anxiety turned to relief when she saw that the beam of the torch was tracing the rough whiteness of a wall, a window frame, and then a wooden door with an iron ring for a knocker.

The torch was flashed upon Yvain, wrapped to her nose and her enormous eyes in the fur laprobe. 'Well, Gretel, we have found a cottage in the woods. Do you suppose Hansel dare use that knocker?'

She gave a chuckle, for she liked it when Don Juan revealed the humour that lurked in him like a vein of gold. 'Gretel's feet are rather cold,' she said.

'I noticed you were limping, child.'

'I lost the heel off my right shoe.'

'Ah, then here goes.' He raised the knocker and brought it down against the door, once, twice, making echoes in the night. They waited, and then they heard someone open an upstairs window. A disembodied voice floated down to them. 'Who is there?' It sounded elderly and querulous.

'*Señora*, we would like to beg of you a shelter for the night. Our car has broken down and we are stranded in the fog.'

'I am sorry, *señor*, but I have not the room—'

'I would pay you well, *señora*.'

There was silence as the woman hesitated, then they heard the window being closed.

'Country people are nervous on nights such as this.' Don Juan spoke in English to Yvain. 'The old woman will take us in if I pay her for her trouble.'

'Tell her who you are,' Yvain suggested.

'For some reason,' a smile lurked in his voice, 'I prefer that we remain strangers to her.'

As Yvain pondered his remark, there was a rattling of bolts being drawn back and the door of the cottage slowly opened to reveal a shawled figure holding a smoky lamp. It was raised so the woman could get a good look at her callers. She peered hard at Don Juan, tall and unmistakably distinguished despite his mist-tousled hair, then she gave her attention to his young, fur-draped companion. She seemed not to recognize the Marqués de Leon, for she said disagreeably: 'I don't know that I should let strangers into my house. How do I know that you are honest people?'

Don Juan took his wallet from his pocket and extracted several bank notes. 'Here you are, *señora*. I trust this will buy us a roof over our heads for the night? Come, the young lady is shivering with the cold.'

The old woman stuffed the notes into her bodice and opened the door just wide enough for Yvain and Don Juan to squeeze past her into the narrow passage. The door banged shut, the bolts were secured, and they were led into the kitchen, where a fire burned low, casting red shadows on the limewashed walls and low smoky ceiling.

Their hostess placed the lamp on a table, and tossed some wood on to the fire. She turned again as the flames leapt to scrutinize her guests, and Yvain thought irresistibly that she was rather witchlike with her sharp eyes and dark, lined face framed in the black head-shawl. She stared at Yvain and said something in rapid Spanish. Yvain glanced helplessly at Don Juan, for she couldn't understand the woman's country dialect.

'The *señora* asks if you would like a bowl of soup.'

'Oh – yes, please.'

He replied to the woman, who went to the fireplace and moved a black pot closer to the flames. All the time she threw remarks over her shoulder, and Yvain felt the sudden grip of her guardian's hands as he removed the fur robe from around her shoulders. The old woman hobbled to the table and began to lay out earthenware soup bowls, spoons and bread.

'What does she say?' Yvain's mist-damp hair clung with a tint of autumn to her temples and her slim neck. She had a fey look, somehow intensified by the lamp shadows and the old-fashioned kitchen with its wooden chairs and three-legged milking stool, the tufted mat in front of the fireplace, and the dresser crowded with china knick-knacks and vases of artificial flowers.

Don Juan's shadow towered to the ceiling ... in his impeccable grey suit he looked very out of place in this rustic kitchen. Yvain was used to seeing him against a background of old-gold drapes and the mellow gleam of antique furniture, the scent of roses mingling with the smoke of his cigar.

He seemed to hesitate, as if he wished to spare her feelings ... which was also unusual.

'The woman says there is only one bedroom ... she is willing to sleep down here in the alcove beside the fire.'

Yvain looked at him and a helpless feeling swept over her. He was leaning rather heavily on his stick, and a tiny nerve was beating beside his mouth. She knew that his leg was aching, and there was nowhere else for him to rest . . . except in that one and only bedroom! She looked away from him and told herself she must not be a prude . . . but what had he told their hostess?

The kitchen was redolent of lentils and herbs as the old woman ladled soup into the bowls. Yvain took her place at the table without daring to look at Don Juan. Her knees felt weak. Her every instinct told her that a stern old Spanish woman would never permit a couple to share a bedroom unless she believed them to be a married couple!

They climbed a narrow flight of cobblestone stairs to the bedroom, the flame of the candlestick Yvain carried lighting up the limewashed walls and the brilliant bedcover as they entered the low-ceilinged room.

There was just a bed, a chest-of-drawers, and a chair. The room was under the eaves and it reminded Yvain of her small, cold bedroom at Sandell Hall . . . but never had that room been shared by a tall, dark man with a gleam of devilry in his eyes.

She caught that gleam in his eyes as he glanced from the single wooden chair to the bed, and she felt sure the silence was filled with the hammering of her heart.

'You seem agitated,' he murmured.

She met his eyes and saw in them the reason for her agitation. Their darkness held that small, satanic smile that made her very unsure of him. 'I always shiver like this when I'm tired.' She tossed her hair back over her shoulder. 'I . . . I'm not being silly because we've got to share this room for the night.'

'We have got to share the bed as well.' He quirked an eyebrow at her. 'I could be a martyr and sit in that uncomfortable-looking chair all night, but I am sure you have too tender a heart to consign me to such discomfort.'

'O-of course not.' She felt weak again and wanted to sink down on the side of the bed, with its crazy quilt and its hand-carved wooden posts. She looked everywhere but at the tall, dark figure of Don Juan, whose face by candlelight had a fascination she didn't dare to notice. She must try not to act jittery because for a few hours they were forced to share a room ... a *bed*!

'I could make do on the chair!' she blurted out.

'*Niña*,' his voice was dangerously soft and low, 'I thought you felt quite safe with me?'

'I do – only—'

'Only what, child?'

'I ... I'm not a child.'

'So that's it! You are old enough to be coy about yourself, and you think that now we are alone like this, I shall lose my self-control and make passionate advances to you.'

Because she was so unsure of him, it was a second or two before she realized that he was being sarcastic. 'I ... I'm not used to this sort of situation, even if you are,' she flashed.

The quirk to his eyebrow grew wicked. 'You are not a child, so I can't spank you for that,' he said lazily. 'But there is another way for a man to deal with a girlish tantrum – can you guess what it is?'

She looked at his mouth and drew as far away as possible from him, the candlelight on her bare young neck and arms, reflecting in her startled eyes, glimmering on the auburn tangle of her hair. The thought alone of being kissed by Don Juan was enough to shatter her composure, and sudden tears of emotion and fatigue shone in her eyes. 'I ... I don't want to fight with you,' she said shakily.

'What do you want, *niña*?' His glance swept over her, taking in her tears and her taut young body. 'Perhaps you hardly know yourself, and I won't taunt you any more tonight. You will sleep beneath the covers of the bed. I shall sleep atop them. Believe me, no sword between a couple was ever as keen as innocence and fear, and you look the picture of both.'

His smile was brief, but while it lasted it was kind, and once again she felt shattered by feelings she hardly understood. One moment she wanted to claw him and run; the next moment he made her want something quite different. If, when he smiled, he had held open his arms to her, she knew she would have run into them and pressed close to him for warmth.

She shivered . . . it could have been her thoughts, or the coldness of the room, but right away he noticed and came limping round to her. He reached out for her hand and felt its coldness. 'Are your feet the same?' he asked.

She nodded. 'Cold feet were always a problem of mine. I used to get chilblains in the winter . . . Sandell Hall was such a big, chilly place.'

'And you had a room without a fire in it, eh?' He pressed her down on to the side of the bed. 'Off with your shoes and I will warm your feet for you.'

It was no use protesting, but without her shoes she felt small, childish, defenceless, and when he took her feet into his hands and chafed them until they tingled, she felt both shy and grateful. It was something a father did for a girl, but this tall man with the dark and enigmatic eyes was in no way paternal. As the warmth from his hands seeped into her, she became drowsy. And when he lifted her legs on to the bed and tucked the covers around her, she gazed up at him with heavy-lidded, wondering eyes.

'Is that better?' he asked, and his shadow was an arc against the wall as he leaned over her and stroked the auburn hair away from her face.

'Mmmm, all nice and tingly,' she said, and the breath seemed to die in her throat as his lean fingers drifted down her cheek. She wanted to turn her head and press her lips against his fingers, but such a gesture might act like a spark to dry tinder and she might find herself in his arms ... at the mercy of his lips hardened by pain, and loneliness, and controlled passion. She shrank away from his touch and at once he turned away from her. Her heartbeats felt as if they must choke her as she lay and watched his shadow against the wall, etched by the candlelight as he removed his shoes, his jacket, his tie and his cuff-links. He placed them on the chair at the bedside, then there was darkness as the candle was snuffed, and Yvain's hand clenched on the quilt as he stretched out on the bed at her side and pulled the laprobe over him.

Yvain heard him breathing, and then he gave a little sigh, as if it felt good to lie down. The long length of his body was close but for the quilt that covered her, and she knew a sense of shock to the roots of her being.

No one must ever know about tonight ... least of all Raquel, with whom he had spent the day. Raquel's eyes were all too eloquent when they rested on him. She would never believe that a girl could spend a night with Don Juan and not find herself in his arms. Yvain thought weakly of those strong arms only inches away from her, and then he murmured: 'Close those wide eyes, *niña mia,* and go to sleep. Tonight is our secret. Tomorrow we will smile about it.'

'What did you tell the old lady?' Yvain dared at last to ask.

'I told her nothing . . . about us.'

'You mean . . . you let her assume that we had the right to . . . share a room?'

'Assumption is the correct word.'

'You really are a bit of a devil, Don Juan!'

'If you choose to think so.' He spoke lazily. 'But you must admit that the bed is more comfortable than nodding in a chair all night.'

'I . . . I suppose so.'

'Then don't let your conscience be a lumpy pillow, Miss Pilgrim. Just look upon me as a draught-excluder and go to sleep.'

She wanted to giggle when he said that . . . she loved him when he gave vent to that humorous side of him . . .

Loved him?

She lay very still and listened to his breathing and felt him move his leg into a more comfortable position. *How do I love thee?* The words drifted through her mind. *I love thee with the passion put to use in my old griefs, and with my childhood's faith – I love thee with the breath, smiles, tears of all my life!*

She closed her eyes and fell asleep beside Don Juan de Leon.

She awoke in the morning before him and found the sun shining into the whitewashed room under the eaves, where birds strutted and broke into song. She remembered at once the events of the night before, and she studied the sleeping face beside her and thought how black was his hair, how proud his nose, how guarded she must now be with this man who was her guardian.

She got out of bed and went to the window. She pushed it wide open and leaned out, breathing the morning air and finding the sun warm after the cold mist of last night. The last little curls of it could be seen among the pine trees, and the moist grasses filled the air with their scent.

If only one could hold on to a chosen moment and never be released from it. Here and now she would choose to be made captive, while the morning was so lovely and she was the only girl in Don Juan's life. No words, no promises already made to others could break the magic spell.

CHAPTER SEVEN

YVAIN was very careful in the days that followed to act as if she had nothing more serious on her mind than her lessons with Señor Fonesca. Each morning the chauffeur drove her into town to the villa, where upon occasion she saw Raquel in the garden, or on her way out to the club to watch the tennis or to lunch with a friend.

The elegant Raquel always wore an air of amusement when she came upon her father's pupil.

'You are an earnest little thing,' she said one morning, when she found Yvain studying at the patio table. 'Manrique Cortez was asking after you only yesterday, and I told him he was welcome to call on you here.'

'I hope he doesn't,' Yvain replied. 'He's distracting and I take my lessons seriously.'

'I can see that.' Raquel clipped a small golden rose and pinned it to the lapel of her beautiful suit. 'Would it not be more fun to marry a nice young man, than to sit poring over those books and filling your mind with a lot of facts and figures?'

'I like to learn, and your father is a wonderful teacher.'

'He is a pet,' Raquel agreed, a hint of possessiveness in her smile. 'There is only one other man I know who can measure up to him for wit and learning and real Spanish charm. Do you find our men charming, Miss Pilgrim?'

Yvain glanced up and found Raquel studying her cool green dress and her auburn hair in a pony-tail. 'Yes, I like to be charmed,' she smiled. 'Latin men certainly have their share of good looks and gallantry.'

'Then it is a wonder you have not fallen in love with

one of them, Miss Pilgrim. Of course, I have heard that the British are a very cool race and not given to revealing what they feel.'

'I feel that I am being given a hint about something, Señorita Fonesca.' Yvain hung on grimly to her smile. 'Please be frank with me.'

'Don Juan cannot always be responsible for you ... is that frank enough? You are not a child even if Juan thinks so.'

'No, *señorita*.' Yvain met the other girl's eyes. 'I wouldn't dream of imposing on Don Juan's generosity for longer than necessary. Your father knows the director of an art gallery in Madrid and I hope quite soon to go and work there as an assistant.'

'Madrid, eh? That should be convenient for you with regard to your friendship with Manrique Cortez. He seems intrigued by you, but take my advice and don't play too hard to get. Men like the thrill of the chase, but they like also to catch up with their quarry.' Raquel smoothed the fingers of her beige gloves. 'Is it possible that you are a little frightened of men?'

'I'm not a shrinking violet,' Yvain protested.

'Manrique seems to think you very modest and shy, and that he may have alarmed you the last time you were alone with him.'

'He annoyed me.'

'My dear,' Raquel looked inquisitive, 'what did he do?'

Yvain thought back to that drive and found its details blurred by the events which had followed at the cottage in the fog. If Raquel should ever learn of that night! How it would shake her self-possession, for she was not the sort to believe that a girl could remain innocent after spending a night with a man. How it would ruffle her

121

poise to believe that Don Juan had an interest in someone other than herself.

If only it were true!

Yvain felt shaken all anew, and she felt also a welling up of rebellion. Raquel was so shallow compared to Don Juan. She spent her days in idle enjoyment, and was not deeply in love with him.

It came as a relief when Señor Fonesca returned to the patio carrying the book of engravings he wished her to study. 'Do you intend to stay and join our studies?' he inquired of his daughter, a twinkle in his eye. 'I thought you were on your way to lunch at the Hidalgo with one of your numerous admirers.'

'He won't mind waiting for me, Papa.' Raquel gave Yvain a pitying smile. 'I feel for you, my dear, that you have to work. You must take my advice and find yourself a husband.'

'Have you yet found one for yourself?' her father asked dryly.

'Yes, Papa, there is someone special.' She smiled mysteriously as she kissed her father on the cheek, and she was still smiling as she waved good-bye at Yvain and walked elegantly from the patio. Her perfume lingered on the air, and her words haunted the rest of the morning for Yvain. That someone special was Don Juan, who must marry to have a son to carry on his name and his guardianship of the Isla del Leon.

Yvain and her tutor lunched beneath a shady tree, while the birds twittered in the sun and the flowers stirred at the attack of the big honey bees.

'You look a little sad, Yvain. Troubled.'

She gave a start and stirred out of her thoughts. 'I was thinking, *señor*, that I can't stay indefinitely at the *castillo*. When do you think I shall be ready to begin work at the gallery in Madrid?'

He smiled as he arose and cut a peach from the wall-tree with a small, ivory-handled knife. 'The young are so impatient for new adventures and fresh faces. Are you tired so soon of your bearded tutor and the thick books he makes you study?'

'No, it isn't that,' she said quickly. 'I enjoy every moment of being here. I lap up all you teach me like a thirsty cat. But I long to be independent ... I can't always take food and board from Don Juan.'

'I am sure he enjoys providing both.' The *señor* stoned the peach and placed half on Yvain's plate. 'Juan is a true Spaniard and very generous. The *Castillo* is also very empty for him and you help to fill it. Come, eat the peach and don't imagine that you are a burden on anyone.'

'When he marries, *señor*—'

'I don't think the great day is imminent, my child.'

'But I want to go away when it happens.'

'That is understandable.' The shrewd eyes were fixed upon her. 'When Juan marries, life will change for you, but in the meantime enjoy being his ward.'

She smiled and ate the peach. '*C'est la vie,*' she murmured.

'Yes, my child, what will be, will be. We must all submit to our destiny whatever it is.'

'Makes me feel as insecure as an autumn leaf.'

'You feel that way, *niña*, because you are young. The young must dream and hope and perhaps be a little melancholy. The best poets and painters were mainly young people, suffering from love rather than finding their comfort in it. Love is at the root of everything ... it cannot be escaped.'

'I've never been in love,' she said. 'I've wondered how

one knows—'

The *señor* studied her for a long moment. 'It becomes a small death each time to say good-bye to a certain person. To walk away when you want only to remain. Love is so basic, *niña*. It is the desire to be part of that person, not for an hour but for every night and day. You will know, believe me, when you fall in love. You are sensitive, and therefore among the truly passionate.'

He laughed quietly at the way she looked at him, her eyes like honey-pools in her piquant face. 'You will either find great joy, or a certain sadness,' he predicted. 'There can be no compromise for the girl who must give everything to one man.'

'You make me sound uncomfortably dedicated,' she half-laughed.

'Without that dedication,' he reached for her hand and lightly kissed it, 'you would not be the perfect pupil.'

'Thank you for the compliment, *señor*. When will you give me my diploma?'

'In good time, *niña*.' His fingers tightened on hers. 'If the marriage of Don Juan becomes imminent, then I shall be among the first to know.'

Yvain hung on to her smile. Of course, Raquel's father would be told at once that he could expect to give his daughter into the keeping of Juan de Leon on a certain day, at the baroque cathedral on the island, with its fretted pinnacles and its sun-mellowed walls. The bride would wear convent-made lace from her head to her heels, and she would carry madonna lilies. The Leon family pearls would grace her throat, and a smile would grace her smooth red lips. The bells would peal, and a day of celebration would be proclaimed all over the island. Everyone would be happy for the Marqués. Everyone would say that he had chosen wisely.

It was several minutes before Yvain realized that Señor Fonesca had left her to take his after-lunch siesta. Their conversation had made her feel restless and she found herself doodling profiles in her notebook ... Latin profiles with a thick sweep of hair above the brow. She threw down her pen and on a sudden impulse let herself out of a side door of the patio and played truant from her studies.

She made her way down the stepped streets to the shore, where fishing-boats and sloops were becalmed in the afternoon sunshine. Few people were about; only cats sloped in the shadows of Moorish archways, and the shutters of the narrow windows were closed against the sun for coolness. The sea air held a tang of fish and roses. A palm tree etched its shadow against a wall, and Yvain was a lonesome figure in her green dress, her hair stroked to an auburn blaze by the hot sun.

Cobbled steps led down to the sandy shore, and there she came upon an upturned boat, its bottom dried by the sun, hiding a crab that scuttled out as she sat down on the bleached hull. It was so quiet. Even the sea was still, and the far off mountains of Spain were like an iron-blue chain across the horizon.

It would surely not be long before she crossed over into the shadow of those mountains and boarded a bus that would drive along roads white with dust, until it entered the city of Madrid, where she would work. She tried to feel excited and hopeful about the future, but when she visualized the loneliness of being alone in a big city, she shrank in upon herself and huddled there upon the hull of the fishing-boat as if she were cold.

It made for coldness to be alone, and it seemed that all her life she must leave what she loved to go somewhere else. She had loved the cottage at Combe St. Blaize, but when her father died she had not been able to stay there. She loved this island and the castle, but when her guardian married she must leave again to go among strangers.

She blinked and felt tears on her lashes. She felt so lonely, and was in the mood to turn in gratitude to the first friendly voice.

When it came she recognized without turning round the velvety inflection of the voice that belonged with a Spanish guitar. 'I was thinking about you, Yvain. My thoughts must have brought me to you.'

She held out a hand to him, wanting his warm clasp to pull her out of the coldness of her thoughts. 'Hullo, Rique. We and the cats are the only ones about.'

He took her hand and drew her fingers through his. His hair was dark like the shadows, his smile was a flash of white like the sun on the walls of the houses terraced above the shore, his touch was warm, and she didn't shrink this time from the daring frankness of his gaze.

'What brings tears to your eyes?' he demanded. 'The sun on the water, or the way you ran away from me for no real reason?'

'As if I'd cry over you!' she scoffed, but her voice was husky and she was pleased to see him. 'Sit down and talk to me, Rique.'

'I intend to.' He sat down beside her on the boat, his legs very long beside hers in narrow dark trousers. His shirt was a hazy blue colour, open at his brown throat. The chain of a medallion shone against his collarbone. He was very Latin and very colourful, and Yvain was girl enough to be warmed by the look of him.

'What did you do after you left me last Sunday? I hope you didn't linger on the beach, for a fog came up.'

How could she forget the fog?

'Don't let us talk about that silly quarrel,' she said in a rather breathless voice.

'It was silly, Yvain. What did I do that was so awful?'

'Please, let's start again from our first meeting. You were very gallant, like a troubadour of old.'

'I prefer how it feels to be young, *pequeña*.' His smile teased her serious eyes. 'What has the Marqués said to you, that you must study your lessons and not encourage the attentions of young men?'

'I want an education, very much.'

'And what are you studying right now? Are you planning to write an essay on fishing-boats?'

'Oh, I'm playing truant,' she confessed. 'All of a sudden I couldn't concentrate, so I ran away from my books for an hour.'

'Lessons, books!' Rique gripped her hand painfully. 'You should be having fun, and if I were the Marqués I would give you lessons of a different sort.'

'Rique!'

He laughed, shamelessly. 'Have you never been to a Spanish wedding, *pequeña*? No? Then I shall take you to one. At six o'clock the couple and their families will go to the church and after the ceremony there will be a party. I have promised to play the guitar, and I have been told to bring a girl.'

He paused and looked her over in her green dress. 'It would give me very much pleasure to take you to the wedding.'

'I'd like to go, Rique, but the car will call for me at four to drive me home to the castle.'

'You can tell the chauffeur that you will be home later.'

'I can,' she agreed. 'But there's Don Juan—'

'Does he lock you in the tower for the rest of the day?'

Rique asked mockingly. 'Are you so under his spell that you dare not please anyone but him? I want to treat you as a woman, Yvain, not as a child. I want to give you music and laughter, not the sombre walls of a castle and a solemn dinner in a room shadowed by memories of the past. He thinks that because he cannot dance, you don't want to. He expects you to be a child all day, and an uncomplaining spinster in the evenings!'

'Rique, what a tirade,' she protested. 'Don Juan is not like that at all. He'd let me go to the wedding if I wanted to.'

'Then there is no problem,' Rique smiled. 'We will return to the villa at four so you can give the chauffeur a message for the Marqués. Then we will go to the Club Hidalgo so I can collect my guitar. I don't work at the club this evening so we are both free to have fun. Don't you think it romantic to celebrate a wedding under the stars?'

'You Latins have a natural aptitude for romance,' she agreed.

'The Spanish girl lives to please the man she likes.'

'I'm afraid nothing will make me Spanish.'

'There you are wrong.' He leaned closer, a gleam in his eyes. 'If you married a Spaniard, then you would become Spanish.'

'At heart I would always be English. I would never have the true *sal española.*'

'You have your own kind of magic.' His eyes travelled over her face and settled upon her hair, tumbling red-brown as autumn leaves against the soft green that sheathed her. Rique's eyes softened, smouldered, and with a murmur in Spanish he pressed her hand against his cheek. 'Cool is the hand of the girl with a warm heart. Last week I wished only to flirt with you. Now I shall treat you differently.'

'No, Rique—' Her heart pounded. 'Let's keep it light-hearted.'

'Like a soufflé,' he promised. 'Like bells and music and moonlight.'

'Rique,' she panicked, 'don't use your charm on me, because I might not be able to resist it. We could both be hurt.'

'That is what life is for, to be hurt, to be healed, to be happy. Yvain, don't fight it.'

How easy it would be not to fight it if fate had let her fall in love with the dark-eyed guitarist. Her smile hurt her mouth, as if it wished to shape itself for weeping. 'Spaniards are so dangerous, because they can be so nice. I'll dance at your friends' wedding. It will be something for me to remember when I leave the island.'

'You do not plan to stay here?'

She shook her head. 'It was always a temporary arrangement. In a while I am going to Madrid to work.'

'Ah, Madrid. There is so much there for me to show you. The old and the modern. The quaint and the beautiful. We shall be happy there.'

She looked at him and wanted to believe that she could be happy miles away from the island of oleander bells and aromatic pine trees, of sunshine on the sea, and turrets against a deep blue sky.

'You look as if it will make you sad to leave the island, Yva.'

Her gaze was upon the tracery of nets and masts along the shore, and then she turned to him with a startled look in her eyes. 'You called me Yva.'

'Don't you like it?'

'Yes, it's friendly.'

'It is more than that, Yva. A diminutive is the sign that a Spaniard accepts you and is fond of you.'

She gave a husky laugh. 'You trapped me into calling you Rique from the start!'

'I hope I have trapped you.' His eyes caressed her and she saw a tenderness in them. She wanted to beg him not to look like that, and her alarm must have communicated itself, for he began to talk of other things. Of his childhood in the hills of Spain, his restless urge to be more than a harvester of almonds and olives. He had run away from home when he was fifteen and hitch-hiked to the city of Barcelona, where he had worked as a waiter and become the pupil of a musician who played the guitar like an angel, but who lived like a devil.

'I have only half the gifts of that man,' Rique mused, 'but I use them to the full and I have ambition. I plan to make a lot of money and when I am rich I shall buy a big house with almond orchards, mimosa trees and fountains. I shall be a man of substance, with a wife and a family.'

Yvain smiled. 'You do surprise me, Rique.'

'You thought me a playboy guitarist, eh?' He gave her hair a tweak. 'I am a Spaniard before I am anything else and we take life seriously even though we sing and make *fiesta* whenever the chance occurs. Tonight you will see us make merry, and I shall teach you to dance like a Spanish girl.'

'Will we go to the church to see the ceremony?' she asked, for his gaiety was infectious and she was beginning to look forward to the wedding.

'*Cara mia*, of course we shall.'

Tall candles burned upon the altar and their light made a halo about the young couple who stood before the priest and murmured their vows. The church tapestries gleamed with silken colours, and the figures of Mary and Joseph were curiously real as they stood beyond the altar; their eyes seemed to rest upon the bridal pair in gentle awareness.

Yvain watched, silent and spellbound, as the bride's white lace mantilla was extended over the shoulders of the young man beside her, a symbolic part of the ceremony, a promise that she would submit to him with love and grace. He then placed upon her hand the wedding ring, and with a shy glance up into his face she slipped a ring upon his hand. The rings of alliance, exchanged now, and waking little sighs of satisfaction among the guests crowding the pews of the church.

The smoke of the candles mingled with the scent of carnations as the priest pronounced the couple man and wife. The dark young man smiled and pressed the hands that held orange blossom, a mother-of-pearl prayer-book and a rosary. They were too shy, too much in love to kiss in public, and Yvain saw the bride's mother raise a handkerchief to the tears in her eyes. For the young bride, her daughter, the marriage vows would be for always. The Latin couple were bound together never to be parted, and they gazed at one another in hopeful trust and joy, the beads of the rosary shining in the glow of the altar candles.

The sun was setting, a blaze of orange and gold, as the guests streamed happily from the church and climbed into the quaint and polished carriages hired by the bridegroom's father. Bells jingled on the harness of the horses as they followed the bridal carriage to the home of the bridegroom. This was an old Iberian farmhouse in the hills, with weathered walls and archways, and a grand old courtyard where lanterns were lit in the dusk, and loops of fairy-lights gleamed among the branches of the cypress and oleander trees.

Flamenco skirts flounced and frothed as young girls were lifted laughingly from the carriages by the men in broad-brimmed hats and smart black suits. Some of the guests rode in on horseback, and Yvain felt as if she were wafted back into another century. The old romantic Spain of sombreros and dashing *caballeros.*

Rique's teeth flashed in a smile as he placed an arm about her waist and led her across the courtyard to be introduced to the parents of the happy couple. Yvain wore a lacy scarf over her hair – a scented, goassamer scarf her tutor had supplied from Raquel's wardrobe – and glances of warm approval were bestowed upon her by the two women in their exotic mantillas draped over high combs set with sparkling stones.

For occasions such as weddings the Latin woman brought out her treasured brooches and necklaces and donned herself with more splendour than the youthful bride. Fans fluttered and dark eyes sparkled. Men with lean, active figures bent over Yvain's hand and murmured in deep voices their pleasure in meeting *la inglesa.* Her heart beat fast with shy excitement and she replied to them in hesitant Spanish and was rewarded by quick smiles of delight that she had taken the trouble to learn their language.

'I find your language, your music and your weddings full of charm,' she smiled, and she could have added that to be among them was to relive again the country dances at Combe St. Blaize. Her father had never left her alone at the cottage; he had carried her across the moors on his shoulders to have fun with the other children at the party.

Here at the wedding party of Doretta and Alvarez,

children were dashing about among the fairy-lit trees, clutching ices and oranges, and dressed in their best frilly dresses and dark suits.

Yvain glanced around her and so much gaiety made her wonder if her guardian was dining alone tonight. Was he alone at the castle, or was he with Raquel, letting the net of her charm and seduction slowly entangle him? How soon before he stood beside a glowing bride to be teased and complimented? Now that she had seen a Spanish wedding, Yvain could imagine vividly the tall, aloof Marqués at the altar, a golden ring agleam in his fingers as he slipped it upon the manicured hand of his bride. A smile would glide over Raquel's lips, for his ring and his vows would make her a Marquesa. She would look the part and act it perfectly, but the symbolism of her lace veil extended over Don Juan's shoulders would have no real meaning for her. She would not submit to him out of a warm and eager love.

'Come, let us go and have some food before I am asked to play and sing.' Rique took her arm and jerked her out of her thoughts. She smiled her agreement and they made their way to the buffet table, which was laden with large platters of food. Coils of crisp bread, sun-cured ham, giant shrimps, various sorts of sausage, country cheeses, slices of pork with stuffing in the centre, chicken legs, and lobsters.

They took plates and made their selection of goodies. Someone poured wine for them from a straw-covered flagon, and as a golden wedge of moon cut its way among the stars, they watched a young man and a girl dance the fandango.

The dance began slowly, almost lazily, and the only sound was the clicking of castanets on the girl's fingers and the stamping of the man's narrow dancing feet.

Slowly their speed intensified, until they were whirling around each other and the girl's colourful petticoats were brushing the narrow trousers of her partner. The music had taken up the pulse-beat of the castanets and the clicking heels, and now and then, like a heart missing a beat, the music paused and the dancers faced each other rigidly. Then it began again and the dance of pursuit and teasing went on, bright skirts whirling, male eyes flashing, a living picture in the light of the lanterns and the stars.

Yvain felt a stirring of her pulses, and there against her shoulder was the lean strength of Rique. His warm breath stirred her hair, loosened from the lace scarf, and she didn't want to think beyond tonight. She didn't want to 'ace the reality of tomorrow.

'Exciting?' he murmured close to her ear.

'Mmmm.' She took a quick sip of wine. 'Thank you for bringing me – I wouldn't have missed all this for the world.'

'You speak as though never again do you expect to attend a Spanish wedding.'

'I might attend one again, but the first time for anything has a kind of magic about it.'

'Like the first time one falls in love?'

She felt his eyes upon her, tiny flecks of lantern light glimmering in their depths. 'I expect the first time is pretty shattering,' she said lightly. 'I wouldn't know.'

'I wonder.' He swung her to face him and tried to read her wide eyes, filled with little lights and shining as if moon-witched. 'All these people think I am courting you. To the Spanish there is no such thing as friendship between a man and a girl – only love, or passion.'

'But we are friends!'

'Don't be a little innocent, Yvain. A friend for a

Spaniard is the fellow with whom he discusses politics and the bullfight over glasses of manzanilla.'

'Did you bring me here on purpose, so everyone would think we were more than friends?'

'Do you mean have I compromised you?' He gave a soft laugh and touched her cheek before she could stop him. 'It would take a little more than that, *chica*. Say I spent a night alone with you and someone was a witness to it, then as a Spaniard I would have to marry you, otherwise you would be a girl with a tarnished name and no other man would want you for his wife.'

'You mean,' her heart beat hard and fast, 'that no one would believe in . . . our innocence?'

'Is it possible that such a night would be innocent?'

'Yes – if the man was a person of honour.'

'He would have to be made of stone,' Rique laughed. 'In any case, it would make no difference if he and the girl had not made love. He would still be obliged to make the girl his wife, or leave her to join the images.'

'The images?' Yvain echoed.

'Yes, a term we have for girls left on the shelf.'

'You really mean that Latin people can be that uncharitable towards a girl whose plight could be brought about by some force beyond her control?'

'Latins have a strict code of honour, and you must remember that it was Eve who tempted the first man. Man is quite a jolly, carefree fellow until a girl takes his eye.'

'You poor men!' Yvain tilted her chin. 'It must be hard on you to be in such danger. Perhaps it would have been better for you if the operation on Adam's rib had not taken place.'

'Quite,' he laughed. 'But think of the fun we would have missed. No sparks, no pretty faces to look at, no kisses. Despite the hazards, it's an agreeable arrangement

'. . . or don't you think so?'

'I think Eve lost us the initiative by doing the tempting. She made Adam think of himself as a prize to be won, and ever since Eden he's acted as if he's the biggest plum in the lottery of life for a girl.'

'For most girls he is,' Rique said shamelessly. 'Come, would you want to go through life without a man to love you?'

Yvain turned to look at the young bridal couple, surrounded by their laughing friends and so poignantly happy tonight that she made an involuntary wish that the realities of marriage would never dim the stars in their eyes. They loved . . . most people wanted to be loved; without it life was empty in so many ways.

It was then that people began to call out to Rique to play for them, and the magic of his music was intensified by the scent of crushed carnations and the glow of lanterns and coloured lights on the Latin faces of the people grouped about the courtyard. A satin frill moved, a bracelet shimmered, white teeth gleamed as a man bent his head to murmur a compliment to a girl with flowers in her shining hair.

Yvain felt welcome among these people, and yet at the same time an onlooker. They were like figures embroidered into some ancient tapestry. Their faces were of the kind that modern living had not moulded into masks of weary cynicism. Their eyes were alert and ardent, and they seemed to put all their hearts into the simple enjoyment of music. They drank it in as if it were wine, and later they all joined hands and made circles and danced the *sardana*. It was all new to Yvain and she loved it, a woman between each man, and all of them ready to show her how to take short steps then long steps, until she caught the rhythm of the dance and felt the joy of it run like wine through her veins.

Did an hour pass, or two, before she found herself alone, fluttering a handkerchief to cool herself, the gilt of the moon in her lifted eyes and the drift of 'Cielito Lindo' through the trees. Tonight she had found a little heaven and almost, but not quite, had blotted out the awareness that soon she must leave this island of warm hearts and sunny days, and nights of witchery.

She breathed the sap in the cypress trees against which she leaned, green-clad like the tree, under the spell of the moon and the music.

Soon the music would die away and Rique would come looking for her. She braced herself against the thought of him, for tonight she was made vulnerable by this beautiful, happy wedding, and if he kissed her, she might be unable to resist him.

He came like a velvet shadow, like a lean panther stalking its prey, and she gave a soft gasp as his arms entrapped her against the tree. She could not retreat from his sparkling eyes, or his lips, that left a medallion of warmth in the soft hollow of her throat. 'A man must keep his eye on you or you vanish,' he murmured against her ear. 'You are fey like your witch-wide eyes, a moth of the night, hardly real even to the touch. It seems a sacrilege to think of you with passion.'

'A little while ago you were telling me to fall in love.'

'I think now that I should like to put you in a slender silver vase and admire you.'

'Up on the shelf?' she laughed.

'Come on,' he laughed with her, 'the bride and groom are about to hand out sweets from the myrtle tree decorated for them.'

Hand in hand they joined the throng of guests, clustering eagerly about the bridal couple to watch while the bride and groom each plucked a sweet for the couple sweet on each other. Yvain was so busy being fascinated by the game that it came as a complete surprise when Doretta presented her with a sweet while Alvarez handed one to Rique. There was a burst of laughter. No one looked surprised but Yvain, and then as she turned to Rique a face in the lantern light caught her attention and she stared in amazement at the woman who had given shelter to Don Juan and herself the night of the fog. She was stunned. Somehow that little old witch of a woman had been part of a dream, blurred in outline like all the other details of that episode and yet unforgettable.

The old woman carried a straw-covered flagon and was serving the guests with wine. She must have been hired to help out at the wedding, and Yvain had been so engrossed by the party that she hadn't noticed her until now.

She smiled tentatively as the woman stared at her. 'Don't be shy, *señorita,*' everyone was calling out. 'Eat the sweet!'

But she couldn't. Her mouth was dry and her heart was throbbing, and she was aware of no one but the black-clad figure with the wine-flagon. 'Can I serve the *señora* with a little wine?' The woman had drawn closer and her dark little eyes were malicious and goblin-like. 'I hope the husband of the *señora* is quite well? Such a gentleman! He paid me well for the night you both spent at my cottage.'

'You make a mistake,' Rique broke in, while those nearby gazed at Yvain with curiosity in their eyes. 'The young lady is not married.'

'No?' The old lady searched Yvain's pale face. 'Then no wonder the gentleman paid me well.'

'What do you mean, old woman?' Rique spoke as if he were breathing fire.

'I would ask the young lady, *señor*.' And like some malignant spirit of mischief the woman was gone, and Yvain gave a gasp of pain as Rique caught at her wrist and hurt the bones with his fingers.

'Did you understand what she said?'

Yvain understood very clearly from his face that her secret – and Don Juan's – was out in the open. 'Yes – some of it.'

Holding her by the wrist and looking murderous, he pulled her away from the party and into a secluded part of the courtyard. 'I should like an explanation, if you don't mind.' His eyes gleamed dangerously in the shadows. 'With whom did you spend a night at the old woman's cottage, and why did you pass yourselves off as husband and wife?'

Yvain tore free of his grip and stood nursing her wrist. 'I'm afraid I can't tell you—'

'You will tell me! I demand to know!'

'And I refuse to tell you.' She was trembling, for suddenly the wedding had lost its appeal for her and she wanted only one thing, to return home to the castle. 'N-no matter what the woman implied, that night at her cottage was totally innocent and the result of circumstances beyond my control or—'

She broke off abruptly, biting back the name that must not be mentioned . . . her guardian's name. No one must know, for only a short while ago Rique had said that a Spaniard who compromised a girl was expected to restore her good name by marrying her!

'I think I should like to leave,' she said tensely.

'No!' He barred her way, making her a prisoner in the small arbour formed by a group of trees. 'We have to

139

talk this out, Yvain. We can't walk away and pretend it never happened. I wish to know the name of this man … only his identity can tell me if the night you spent with him was as innocent as you say. I want to believe in your innocence.'

'That's generous of you.' She felt a midnight breeze touch her bare arms with a ghostly coolness. 'But with typical male arrogance you lay down conditions before proving your generosity. I'm sorry, Rique. I can't tell you the name of my partner in adversity, so you will have to think what you like—'

'Was it Don Juan, by any chance?'

For a petrified moment she thought she betrayed herself with a cry, but in actuality she stood rigid with shock. She had to make a physical effort to speak. 'Really, what a thing to say! If Don Juan wished to seduce me, he would hardly need to take me to someone else's house for the night!' She shrank from Rique, pained by the words he had forced from her.

'Then who … ?' Rique's voice was a growl, and he stood tensed in front of her, as if ready to spring at her and shake from her the name of the man she protected. 'Who else on this island do you know? What other man apart from Señor Fonesca?'

'Are you now accusing my tutor?' The coldness gripping her limbs had crept into her voice. 'Rique, does it matter? Won't you believe that nothing happened that was wrong?'

'Why do you shield the man so obstinately?'

'You are the obstinate one, Rique.' She drew a sigh. 'You forget the Sunday we had a driving date and we quarrelled. I – met someone else. Someone you wouldn't know.' It was a wild half-truth, a desperate attempt to cover up for her guardian, to keep him unexposed to scandal. The strict moral code of these people had the perverse effect of creating scandal, and the last thing on earth she wanted was to blacken Don Juan de Leon in their eyes. He was no saint, but he stood as an example of honour and courage and courtesy, and he might consider himself honour bound to marry her if scandal ever linked them together.

She met Rique's eyes in the moonlight and saw the baffled anger and disillusion reflected in them. 'Forgive me for shattering your illusions about me.' She attempted to speak lightly. 'You must believe that nothing more terrible happened than that we got stranded in the fog that came down and took shelter beneath the first roof we could find. He was gallant and kind and I shall always be grateful to him.'

'Are you in love with him?'

The question took her breath away . . . she had to fight not to betray her agitation. 'One can't love a stranger.' She forced a laugh. 'It would be too shattering an experience. But I shan't find it easy to forget him.'

'I can't understand how you could allow a stranger to masquerade as your – husband!'

'The old woman assumed it . . . he thought it wouldn't matter in the circumstances.'

'How very short-sighted of him,' Rique snapped. 'That old woman has seen you again and let the cat out of the bag. All my friends will think you an adventuress.'

'Are you so swayed by what everyone else thinks?' She studied his face in the moonlight, stern and young and rather hurt, like that of a boy who had found a defect in a toy he had grown fond of. 'You're really a very strait-laced Latin beneath your air of flirtation, aren't you, Rique? Well, it looks as if I shall have to make the most of being banished to the shelf.'

'Don't make a joke of it!'

'It is rather amusing,' she smiled wryly. 'To be thought a scarlet woman when only a few weeks ago I was a wallflower, tagging along in the wake of a woman who thought of no one but herself. I wonder what she'd say? That I should have kept my hair in a bun, I suppose.'

'Yvain,' he gripped her shoulders and shook her, 'scandal spreads like a bush fire around an island and already people will be whispering about you. Don't you care?'

She cared far more that Don Juan should not be found out as the man who had shared that cottage bedroom with her. He had been strangely kind to her, and her heart moved at the thought of him and she wanted to repay him for the things he had given her, especially these weeks of study with Raquel's father. She thought of his romance with Raquel ... and wanted in an instant not to think about that.

'I should like to go home,' she said. 'It's past midnight and some of the other guests are leaving.'

Rique seemed poised on the edge of impulsive words, and then he compressed his lips and looked at her face raised to his, a little sad and appealing, the moon in her eyes, her hair tousled about her shoulders from the dancing. Only a little while ago they had been enjoying the *sardana*, and the bride and groom had plucked the sweetheart sweets for them. Now it was ended. The sweetness had turned bitter on Rique's lips.

They said their farewells and left the *finca* in the car of a friend. It was a great relief to Yvain when the turrets of the castle came into view, moonlit and brooding on their hilltop. She felt like Cinderella who had gone to the ball so gaily, and who returned home in tears.

'Good night...' The words floated back over her shoulder as she ran to unlock the side door of the *castillo*. As she closed it behind her, Rique and his friend drove away.

CHAPTER EIGHT

THE butterfly lamps glimmered low in the patio as Yvain stole across to an archway that led into the castle. Moths glimmered green among the trees and a frog was croaking in the basin of the fountain. The shining slipper of a moon glided through the sky and made ghostly a pergola hung with blossom. The moonlight was cool, a cloak of silver in which she stood for a moment, part of the night and its mystery.

And then as she stood there she heard the sound of a piano being played in the castle. The music stole out softly into the night, sad and enchanting, and as if drawn by the sound she followed until she came to the partly open door of the golden room. She paused and listened and it was so late, and the castle was so still, that a ghost might be in there – the room of Rosalita – playing the Chopin prelude. So lonely, heard in the stillness of the night, so that Yvain hesitated to look into the room.

Her heart drummed softly, and then at last she found her courage and took the few steps that made it possible for her to see the pianist. The candelabrum was alight on the piano top and the twin flames moved, making jewels of the crystal drops and playing shadows over the profile of her guardian.

He played on as if unaware of her, but she knew his instincts were too alert not to have sensed a presence. She felt instinctively that he was displeased with her. The quickening of her heart told her he had been waiting for her to come home. Though he wore a dark silk dressing-gown with a silk cravat tucked in at the neck, his hair was smooth and unruffled and it was obvious he had not been to bed.

As the prelude drew to a close, the tumult of her pulses made her feel a little faint. She wanted to retreat from him, but she couldn't move. She wanted to speak, but the words wouldn't come. She would do anything, kneel at his feet, if he wouldn't treat her as a child who had stayed out too late and must be punished with a reprimand.

There was silence in the room, and then he turned slowly to look at her, dark, stern, shaking her heart. His features had a taut and chiselled look, a certain pallor intensified by the dark silk of the robe and the cravat. His eyes were too compelling to be evaded. They held hers and she saw the shimmer of anger in them.

'Are you aware of the time?' he asked bitingly.

'I ... I know it's late.' Her voice held a tremor. 'I've been to a wedding ... it was a late ceremony and then there was a party and we didn't leave until after midnight ...'

'We?' His voice went dangerously soft. 'I take it you mean yourself and Manrique Cortez?'

'Yes, *señor*.'

'The wedding was so gay and colourful that you couldn't bear to leave, eh? There was wine and music, and the dancing. I can tell from the look of you that you enjoyed the dancing.'

'I loved the dancing.' She put a hand to her lips as if to still the shake in her voice. 'Is it wrong, Don Juan, to enjoy a wedding party? Am I so young and foolish that I can't be trusted anywhere but here or at my lessons?'

His eyes flicked her face, her dress, the lace scarf draping her shoulders. 'You are too young to be out until the small hours. Now please come in and close the door. I wish to be told, Yvain, to whose wedding you have been.

I gather they were friends of Cortez?'

'They were the nicest couple!' Colour warmed her cheeks as she obediently shut the door and stood in a defensive attitude before him. 'The party was held at a *finca* in the hills belonging to the father of Alvarez, a Señor Velarde.'

'Ah, so, a man of good name around the island. I am gratified that Cortez took you among people I can approve of. I have heard that he is not always so particular.'

'You are being pompous!' Yvain exclaimed. 'I'm not a convent-bred *señorita* who has to be guarded against life. You are forgetting, *señor*, that I worked as a maid and lived back-stairs, and that I waited on the guests who came to the parties at Sandell Hall. It made a nice change to be a guest at a party tonight!'

'I am pleased that you enjoyed yourself, but as your guardian I am permitted some anxiety when you are late coming home.'

She studied his face by candlelight, but he didn't look anxious to her, only stern and annoyed. 'You had no need to wait up for me,' she said stiffly. 'Unless you felt that I needed a reprimand.'

'I'm not reprimanding you, child.'

'It feels like it.' She gave way to a wry little smile. 'Your frown is so black that my knees feel weak. If you go on looking so grim I shall probably collapse on the carpet with fright!'

His lips twitched, a sign that he was relenting. 'I suppose I forget what it is to be young and in company that makes one forget the time. I forget that you have never been to a Spanish wedding and that you must have found it fascinating. Tell me,' he shifted his leg and gripped the ebony stick that was never far from his hand, 'what part did you enjoy the most?'

Her thoughts ran back over the evening and she remembered the candles on the altar, the white lace extended over the bridegroom's shoulders, and the exchanging of the marriage rings. 'The ceremony itself, Don Juan.' Suddenly, with the grace of the young, she knelt and slipped a stool under his left leg. He stared down at her and she felt lost in the dark depths of his eyes. 'Why did you do that?' he asked.

'I think your leg is giving you pain,' she replied, kneeling before him with the skirt of her dress like a green pool around her, her hair falling rain-straight around the stem of her neck, her face upraised to him, pale in the candle-light, with the shyness in her eyes because at last she had dared to talk about his pain.

'You are perceptive,' he drawled.

'You are too proud – always – to admit what hurts you, señor.'

'I would become a bore, Yvain, if I groaned each time this limb of mine chose to be awkward. I have learned to to live with it, and you must not pamper me.'

'We should all be pampered now and then,' she smiled. 'Shall I pour you a glass of wine?'

'Yvain,' he leaned forward and his long fingers caught at her wrist and she was shocked by her instant reaction ... the thrill that ran into her very bones. 'You are not to think of yourself in servitude, ever again. You owe me nothing, least of all your sympathy. Do you understand?'

'Yes, I understand.' She drew a shaky breath. 'I can take things from you because you have the money, but you refuse the bit of gratitude I have to give in return. It isn't much, but it's all I have to give.'

He smiled strangely when she said that. 'One might take you for a Latin girl when your eyes flash. You will find in that cabinet over by the windows a decanter of pale gold wine. King Cophetua will be pleased to take a glass with his beggar maid.'

Her eyes grew very wide as they dwelt on his lean face with its slightly wicked smile. 'Oh – yes!' She jumped to her feet and went to the cabinet that stood between the long silken curtains at the windows. There were gilded dragons on the doors that swung open to reveal an array of antique decanters and long-stemmed goblets, and Yvain busied herself with the wine pouring, and collected herself.

It had swept through her like a storm that Don Juan de Leon would be devastating if he ever loved a woman beyond thought or reason. She could not believe that he loved Raquel Fonesca in such a way. Raquel would not be so restless if he did, seeking gossip and the pleasure of being admired by other men on the terrace of the Club Hidalgo. She would be content ... happy beyond anything to bask in the love of the lion of the island.

Yvain held the goblets by their stems and crossed the room to her guardian, and as she felt his dark Latin eyes upon her she was afraid she would spill the wine, or trip and shatter the glasses. He was so real he made her nervous, and yet at the same time he was part of the dream she would carry away with her. She would remember him here, so much a part of the haunting fascination of the room of golden mirrors, the piano with its carved frame, the panels of Latin figures painted on a gold background.

'Here you are, *señor*.' She handed him his glass of wine and watched the curving of his long hand around the bowl, his touch upon the cut-glass facets with fingertips that were so alive. His hands loved beauty, and could make beauty, and she wanted again to listen to his playing.

'I wish you would play something else before I have to run away to bed,' she murmured.

'Have you not heard enough music for one night?' His eyes held hers as he sipped his wine. 'I am sure Cortez played his guitar to you, and there is no other musical instrument that voices so well the mood of the moment, or the temperament of Spain.'

Her eyes dwelt on the guitar that hung by scarlet ribbons beside the portrait of Rosalita. She could imagine him as a boy, seated at his mother's knee, listening as she played and sang to him of the land they had run away from. . . .

'What would you like to hear?'

She looked at him and knew that it must be something she would never forget. 'Play me something you are fond of, *señor*.'

'Very well, Yvain.' He set aside his wine glass, and she went and curled herself around the cushion of an armchair. Her heart beat fast from the wine and the strange enchantment of being alone like this with Don Juan. She closed her eyes as he began to play, and it was just the music she would have chosen, lovely and sad, with the sadness of lovers who must part.

He played the love theme of Tristan and Ysolde, and all through it Yvain sensed in the room the haunting presence of his mother. In her loneliness Rosalita had made this room her retreat from the coldness of her in-laws. Here she had waited for her husband to return to her from Spain, and at last she had run away to join him and in the hills they had fought together as partisans. In the hills he had died and she had taken her son far, far away. She had taught him to love music . . . but she had taught him also to be wary of love.

Yvain looked at the portrait and the passionate dark

eyes seemed to meet hers. They seemed alive and aware, as if to say that to love too much was to court heartache and that Yvain had better take heed before she found her own life made unhappy by a love she was not born to have.

The music died softly away and Yvain became aware that there were tears in her eyes. She blinked them quickly away as Don Juan turned to look at her. His eyes were the eyes in the portrait. The music he had played had been about a forbidden love. Perhaps in his subtle way he told her that she must leave him as she had come to him, as a waif of the night.

'Did you like the music I chose for you?' he asked.

She nodded. 'It was beautiful, *señor*, like the moment in church when a corner of the bride's veil was draped over her husband's shoulder. Something very special to remember.'

'Do you know what that part of the ceremony implies?' His head and shoulders were dark against the candlelight, and his face was shadowed so that she couldn't read his expression.

'I think it means that the bride submits herself to her husband's authority. It seemed to mean something like that and was somehow so beautiful, the white lace against his dark suit and her dark hair, binding them together.'

'The Latin vows are eternally binding, Yvain. On earth, in heaven, whether together or apart. Because of this a man must be very sure, and the girl must not be blinded by the things outside of love. She must feel more than admiration or affection for the man; more than gratitude because he may have been kind to her. Love is more pain than delight . . . in the beginning.'

Yvain could not read his expression, for in that moment one of the candles went out as if someone blew upon it. But if he spoke of love as a painful delight then he felt it, had been caught by it, and would marry for more than a son to carry on the tradition of his name. He would marry for his own sake, because he wanted the woman beyond anything else on earth.

The room felt suddenly cold and Yvain gave a shiver. The wine had left its tears in the stemmed glasses, petals had fallen from the roses for Rosalita, and the candles were dying. She uncurled out of her chair to her feet. 'How late it must be, *señor*! I shall be falling asleep over my lessons tomorrow.'

'Yes, it is about time we both went to bed.' He reached for his stick, but as if possessed it slid away from his hand and fell with a clatter to the floor. In an instant Yvain ran forward to pick it up. She held it out to him with a smile that was instantly banished by the look he gave her as he took it. A dark, savage look, as if he could have struck her with it.

She backed away from him, bewildered and afraid.

'Go to bed!' He gripped the stick as he towered to his feet.

'Won't you say good night?' The words trembled on her lips, for he looked so angry, as if he couldn't bear to be helped by her.

'Good night.' He turned away from her. 'In future keep your pity under control and don't leap to retrieve the things I drop as if I'm a doddering invalid!'

'I'm sorry.' She felt bruised by his words, and tears were choking her as she ran out of the room and made for the stairs that led to her room. He wasn't kind at all! He was proud and cruel and she wanted to leave his house! She wanted to go miles away, and tomorrow she would ask Señor Fonesca to arrange for her to go to Madrid as soon as possible. There she would have a job. She would be independent. She could try at least to forget her devil guardian when she was far away from him.

She slept fitfully and was glad when morning came. To her relief Don Juan did not join her for breakfast on the patio, and by nine o'clock she was on her way by car to the Villa Fonesca.

As she was let into the house, Raquel came to her across the cool tiles of the hall, looking rather agitated. 'Papa is not well and has the doctor with him,' she said. 'Yvain, you will have to return to the castle. I cannot have you under my feet while I am looking after my father.'

Yvain was instantly concerned for her tutor. 'I am sorry, Raquel! I thought he looked rather tired yesterday, but it was a warm day and I put his fatigue down to the heat.'

'On and off he has complained of a pain in his side.' Raquel made a significant gesture with her hands. 'The doctor has warned him about lifting those heavy books he has in the library, now he has gone and strained his heart and must rest for a week or so.'

'Poor Señor Fonesca.' Yvain looked troubled. 'Is there anything I can do to help? I'm so fond of him and—'

'My dear,' Raquel became beguiling, 'there is a favour you can do for me. You can take a note for me to Señora Grayson, the American woman who invited me to lunch with her today on board her yacht. I hate to let anyone down and she is rather charming.'

Raquel turned to an elegant writing-table in the hall and Yvain watched as she wrote her note of apology. She was as concerned at breaking a lunch date as she was about her father, and Yvain felt like reminding her that a girl's father was a very special person and that no one could ever take his place. No other man in a girl's life was ever as gentle and understanding. No other love was ever as secure and undemanding.

'Here you are.' Raquel handed to her a sealed envelope. 'The Señora Grayson's yacht is the *Blue Dolphin*. It's anchored about a mile off the island and one of the fishermen will row you out to it. Such an elegant craft, and I was so looking forward to being shown over it. The *señora* did drop a hint about a cruise . . .'

'A sea trip would certainly be good for your father,' Yvain murmured.

'Yes . . . of course.' Raquel half frowned as she glanced towards the stairs. 'I must go up to him.'

'Please tell him that I wish him better, Raquel. And that I shall miss our lessons.'

'He should not be giving lessons.' Raquel spoke sharply. 'Lifting those heavy books has caused him to be laid up.'

Yvain bit her lip. 'I shan't be taking many more lessons with the *señor*. I meant to speak to him today about my job in Madrid. I feel I'm about ready to tackle it.'

'Do you mean you wish to leave the island?' A gleam of speculation came into Raquel's eyes. 'Are you not happy at the castle? Juan has been most generous to you, but I suppose it means less to a girl when she knows that a man's kindness is not motivated by any personal feeling. Juan is charitable by nature.'

Yvain winced, for Don Juan's charity was the last thing on earth that she wanted. She tucked Raquel's note into the hip pocket of her cream slacks, and tried to look as jaunty as her orange sports shirt. 'I'll call in tomorrow if I may, to see how the *señor* is feeling?'

'If you wish to do so,' Raquel said coolly. 'Do assure Señora Grayon that I am most sorry to break our date, but I must be a dutiful daughter and remain with my father.'

'Not every girl has such a fine father,' Yvain said meaningly. 'I wish him a speedy recovery, *señorita. Hasta mañana.*'

She went out again into the sunshine and made her way down the cobbled streets to the harbour. It was a morning when everything had a peachy tinge and she felt so sorry that Señor Fonesca was confined to his bed. He loved the beauty of this island, hidden away from the world so that the old myths and sorceries were still believed in. She felt the sun on her arms as she crossed the plaza, with its baroque fountain and the cluster of houses with flower-hung balconies. Melons were being sold from a stall near the church; she paused to buy a slice and it tasted cool and juicy as she made for the tracery of nets and masts along the shore.

She was looking for a boatman who looked idle enough to want to earn a little rowing money. It was a good thing she had some pocket money, for Raquel had not thought to pay for the errand on which she was sending her.

Yvain spotted a youth leaning against a palm tree near a beached canoe. He had the sun and wind attractiveness of a seafarer and she approached him and asked if he could row her out to the *Blue Dolphin,* whose elegant blue and white shape could be seen at anchor about a mile off-shore.

He flicked a look over her casual attire and her hair in a sunlit switch down over her shoulder. 'The *señorita* has friends on the yacht?' he asked.

'I have a message for the lady who owns the yacht,' she explained. 'And I would like to be rowed back to the island after I deliver it.'

He nodded and began to pull the canoe down to the water. He held the small craft steady while Yvain climbed in and sat down on the plank seat. She felt a momentary pang of fear as the paddles dipped and they began to pull away from the safety of the beach. Then her fear was lost in the beauty of the bay and in the cool sea breeze fanning her face and throat. The water was so blue that she almost expected it to drip in shades of blue from her fingertips. Seabirds were etched against the sky and the tanned face of the young fisherman was capped by dark, salty curls.

'We don't get many tourists to our island,' he said. 'They are not encouraged by the Marqués, who wishes the island to remain unspoiled.'

'I hope the Marqués doesn't think that I spoil the island for him,' she said, with a rather wistful smile.

'Ah no!' The bold young eyes appraised her. 'If all tourists looked like the *señorita*, then I am sure the Marqués would be delighted.'

'I wonder?' She gave a little laugh that held a little sadness, and saw that they were drawing near to the *Blue Dolphin*. A sailor came to the rail of the yacht and stood watching their approach.

'Ahoy there!' He had a Yankee twang in his voice and he wore white ducks, a navy jacket and a yachting cap pushed to the back of his fair head. He leaned over the side as the canoe drew nearer and Yvain waved the letter to indicate that she wanted to deliver it.

'Come aboard!'

She hesitated, for there was a bit of a swell around the yacht and the flimsy canoe was rocking. She had to keep her balance in order to step from the canoe to the iron rungs leading to the deck, and she had visions of plunging into the water.

'Climb up and don't look down,' came yet another call from the gangway, and because there had to come a time when she must lose her fear of the sea, she grasped the cool iron and swung herself upwards. It was easier than she had imagined and the salty sea breeze could not play games with the slacks she was wearing. As she reached the deck, strong hands lifted her the rest of the way, and she gave a breathless laugh and met a pair of sea-blue eyes.

'We-ll, this is a surprise!' He looked her over. 'Don't tell me the island has its mail delivered by the local cuties?'

Her eyes filled with amusement, for he seemed unaware that she was English and she handed over the envelope with a few demure words in Spanish.

'From Doña Raquel?' He looked at the envelope as if he longed to tear it open. 'For my mother, eh?'

'Señor Fonesca is not at all well and Raquel thought it best that she stay with him. She's disappointed about missing her trip to the yacht.'

'Huh?' He stared at Yvain and then gave a laugh. 'So you're not a *señorita*! You're a tourist like me?'

The word had a way of going through her like a knife, but it was true ... she was only a tourist who had fallen in love with the island. She couldn't stay, like the young fishermen, like the women collecting seaweed on the shore, or the pupils of the convent out walking with the nuns in their great wimples.

'The Isla del Leon is quite a place.' Mrs. Grayson's son stood at the deck rail gazing towards the island with its white cluster of houses, its tall palms and bell-tower above the wharves. 'Are you staying with the Fonescas? Raquel didn't mention having a guest—'

To Yvain's relief she was spared an explanation of where she was staying, for at that moment a woman appeared on deck. She was plump, grey-fair, and dressed pleasantly in cool pink. 'Kent, who have we got calling on us?' She approached with an inquiring smile, and then her blue eyes widened as they dwelt on Yvain. 'Well, my, this is an honour! I saw you only the other day and it was pointed out to me that you're the ward of the Marqués de Leon. The little girl with a name out of a fairy tale!'

Yvain winced and felt like making a dash for the gangway.

'Yvain and the Lion!' Mrs. Grayson said triumphantly. 'How too quaint and wonderful to meet you, my dear. Do I take it you're a friend of Kent's?'

Kent was looking highly amused as he handed Raquel's note to his mother. 'The young lady brought this.'

She opened the envelope, read the enclosure, voiced her regret that Señor Fonesca was not feeling well, and then announced that if Raquel could not join them for lunch, then Yvain must take her place.

'But I couldn't—' Yvain wanted to escape all questions regarding Juan de Leon, and there was a deep gleam of curiosity in Mrs. Grayson's blue eyes.

'I insist, my dear.' Bettina Grayson was a woman unused to being denied. 'I'll only let you go if you have to meet the Señor Marqués for lunch.'

Yvain was tempted to tell a white lie, but honesty prevailed and she admitted that she wasn't expected home. 'All the same, I have some lessons I should be getting on with.'

'Lessons?' Mrs. Grayson raised her eyebrows. 'Language lessons, my dear?'

'Yes.'

'Oh, they can surely wait. Kent and I would love to have you to lunch and I'm not going to take a refusal.' Mrs. Grayson looked at her son in a charmingly bossy fashion. 'We'll have drinks brought to the sun-deck, Kent. I'm longing to get really acquainted with our fairy-tale girl.'

'A boy brought me to the yacht in his canoe.' Yvain avoided a direct meeting with Kent Grayson's amused eyes. 'He's waiting to take me back to the island.'

'I'll go and tell him that you won't be going back – not yet awhile,' said Kent with a smile.

CHAPTER NINE

YVAIN found in the next few days that she was seeing Kent Grayson rather a lot. He was pleasant company, and while Señor Fonesca was laid up she was free to roam about the island with Kent. He had a high-powered camera and was a keen photographer and together they found old and lovely places to put on film.

He was naturally curious about the castle, but Yvain made excuses about taking him there to meet her guardian. 'Don Juan doesn't regard his home as a tourist attraction,' she said.

'But I'm a friend of yours,' Kent wheedled, 'and you're his ward. Surely I can come home with you to be introduced to him?'

'He likes his privacy.'

'Are you scared of him?' Kent took a picture of her as she sat on a wall beside a golden allamanda tree.

'Of course not!'

'You look as if you are, honey. Is he the traditionally stern and black-browed guardian who rules you with a rod of iron?'

She gave a laugh and plucked a spray of blossom. 'He's the handsomest man in the world, and if his temper is uncertain, it's because he has had sadness in his life and the torturing pain of almost losing his leg in a riding accident. He loved to ride and was a *gaucho* when he was a young man.'

'How old is he now?' Kent lounged against the wall and lit a cigarette. As he puffed smoke he narrowed his eyes and they were like shafts of blue upon her face.

'He's about thirty-five.' She stroked the golden spray against her cheek and looked very young herself, and uncertain of the future. Until her tutor was well, she could not talk to him about the job he had in mind for her.

'Somehow I got the impression he was older.' A smile quirked on the edge of Kent's lip. 'So he's handsome, eh? It's a wonder you haven't got a crush on him. I have heard it said that Latin men have a lot of S.A.'

'Spanish appeal?' she smiled.

'You know what I mean, Miss Pilgrim.' Kent leaned forward and tweaked her braid, reminding her of Rique and making her shy away from the touch. Kent grinned. 'You shy of men, Yvain?'

'I like to be friends with them,' she rejoined.

'Because it's more comfortable?'

'I see no point in flirting with every man one meets.'

'You think certain aspects of the man-woman relationship should be kept sacred, eh? For the one and only?' Kent's blue eyes held a quizzical light. 'Have I actually met up with an old-fashioned, heart-thinking girl who could love a guy for more than the security he has to offer?'

'Kent, not all women are mercenary!'

'The kind I've met have wanted to feather their nest rather than make a love nest.'

'You escaped getting caught by one of them, so I think you're a wily bird, Kent. You know what you want.'

'Maybe I want someone like you?' He spoke lightly but with a glint in his eyes. 'Are you heart-free, Yvain?'

'Yes, and I'm staying that way.' She slid off the wall and they made their way to a beach *taberna*, where the tables were shaded from the sun by thatched umbrellas.

Walking in the sun had made them both dry and Kent

ordered a couple of long iced fruit drinks and told the waiter to bring them a menu in about a quarter of an hour. The sea sparkled only a few yards from where they sat, and a lazy band of seabirds mewed and frolicked on the crest of the waves.

It was pleasant to sip a cool drink in the company of an attractive man, and Yvain was not unaware that she was drifting into a relationship that could offer more than Rique's passion; less than the stormy enchantment she dreamed of.

She liked Kent and found him good company. His mother was a charming, good-hearted, inquisitive woman. Only last evening, as they had sat dreaming away an hour on the starlit deck of the yacht, Mrs. Grayson had hinted that Yvain would make the perfect companion. Soon they were leaving to sail on to Spain, then Portugal, and home to America. Yvain could go with them . . . if she chose.

'Come back from far away.' Kent took her hand and pressed the slender fingers. 'I felt awful lonely just then, as if I had no place in your thoughts.'

'But I was thinking about you.' She gave him a thoughtful smile. 'I shall miss you, Kent, when you sail away.'

'Sail away with me,' he coaxed. 'Mom likes you. You could take the companion job she broadly hinted at, and we could let things develop nice and easy between us. If they didn't develop – not for lack of encouragement on my part, be warned – then what would you have lost? You told me you expected to leave the Isla del Leon to go and work in Madrid. What, all alone?' His fingers tightened on hers. 'A girl like you? A tawny kitten with a lost look in her eyes. There is, Yvain! Makes me wonder who put it there.'

'I'm just hungry for some big delicious shrimps.' She gave a laugh. 'Snap your fingers like a Spaniard and let's have a look at the menu.'

'I'm not a Spaniard, honey.'

Her eyes dwelt on his close-cut fair hair, took in the sea-blue gaze, the sudden compression of his lips. 'No, there's nothing Latin about you, Kent.'

'Does it make a difference?'

'On the contrary, it makes me feel ... secure.'

'On solid ground with no fireworks underneath, eh? No hidden volcano?'

She laughed again, ignoring the jab of pain at the memory of the stirring of the volcano in Don Juan. The anger when she had picked up his ebony stick. The biting order that she keep her pity to herself. Pity? She had never felt any such thing for a man so strong, so adult, so independent. She had only wanted to give him a little of her heart's warmth.

Kent sat back, his glass in his hand. 'The solid people have more to offer in the long run than the mystery people you can never get really in touch with. I think if you come away with us, if you leave this island without looking back, you will find happiness.'

She gazed first at Kent and then at the distant mountains of Spain, peaks of violet above the blue and gold of the horizon. 'Going to Madrid was all so settled in my mind, until you came.' She glanced back at Kent. 'Racquel's father has been helping me to learn about art and antiques. I wanted a career.'

'There are art galleries in California, and I'd be there, Yvain.'

'You Americans are very persistent salesmen.'

'There are orange valleys and white-stoned houses. You'd love it there.'

'Do you and your mother live in a white-stoned house, Kent?'

'We do.' His smile was slow and attractive. 'It has a couple of patios and some camellia trees. They bloom scarlet. Quite a picture against the white walls.'

'I,' she gave a sigh of uncertainty, 'I couldn't decide anything without talking it over with my guardian.'

'Only a temporary guardian, Yvain. He doesn't own you.'

'No—'

'Does he act as if he owns you?'

'No, but he's been good to me. I had nothing when I was fished out of the sea and brought here by boat. He arranged with the Spanish authorities that I stay here as a visitor. He sent to Madrid and ordered some lovely clothes for me. He persuaded Señor Fonesca to become my teacher. I . . . I was only a maid-companion. He treats me almost as a . . . niece.'

'Not a daughter?'

'He's hardly old enough for that.' She smiled slightly. 'Unless as a young *gaucho* he was very precocious.'

'I'd like to meet him, Yvain. I feel I should in the circumstances.' Kent spoke seriously. 'I think you're half inclined to accept Mom's offer of a job, and if I speak with the Marqués he will at least be in no doubt about the kind of people we are. I gather this other woman you worked for was a bit of a tartar?'

'She was all tartar.' Yvain smiled and shrugged. 'Maybe I allowed myself to be put upon, but mixing with Spanish people has taught me that pride doesn't have to be overbearing, and that everyone is really equal. Not once during my stay at the castle have I heard or seen Don Juan anything but gracious towards his staff. He's aloof because that's his way, but he isn't a bully.'

'Will you take me to see him?'

'Kent, let's wait a day or two—'

'But we leave on Saturday! We're only staying till then so we can take in the fun of the *fiesta* on Friday.' Kent frowned. 'You've got to make up your mind, Yvain. Somehow I get the impression that if the Señor Marqués says no to anything, then you go along with it.'

'Not all the time,' she protested.

'When have you ever defied him?'

'There was Rique – my guardian was not keen on my friendship with him, and I found out later that Don Juan is much more clear-sighted about people than I am. Or maybe I should say more worldly.'

'Who's Rique?' The blue eyes looked jealous.

'He's the guitarist at the Club Hidalgo.'

'He's too good-looking not to have a roving eye,' Kent grunted.

'Yes.' She laughed a trifle nervously, and remembered with a missed heartbeat the last time she and Rique had met and why they had parted. She looked at Kent, who had been her constant companion for several days, and suddenly she felt a little afraid. People might already be talking about them. They might be saying that he was the man with whom she had spent a night alone. If the gossip reached Kent's ears, would he react as Rique had done?

'Hungry?' He smiled across at her. 'Shall we order those big delicious shrimps?'

She nodded and he called the waiter to their table. He was nice. She felt at ease with him, and California was a long way from the island. All those miles would surely blur the memory of Don Juan, until she could think of him as happily married to Raquel and no longer alone.

The shrimps were big, dewy and pink, and with them they had twists of Spanish bread and a carafe of white wine. Kent then had veal cutlets, while Yvain toyed with a ham salad. She no longer felt very hungry. It seemed to her that the sea had lost some of its sparkle and the mewing of the birds sounded a little sad. But things always seemed that way when you knew you were seeing them for perhaps the last time. If she left on Saturday with Kent and his mother, then already this place, this moment, were turning into memories.

After lunch they lazed on the beach beneath the shade of a palm tree. They didn't talk much. It was as if Kent understood that quietly and a little sadly she was easing the island out of her heart. Preparing herself for the moment when she would say good-bye, and her Spanish guardian would say *Vaya con Dios*.

Kent invited her to spend the evening of the *fiesta* on board the yacht, which was being decorated with coloured lights for the festive occasion.

'Do you think the Señor Marqués would agree to attend our small farewell party?' Mrs. Grayson asked hopefully. 'I saw Doña Raquel this morning and her father is so much better that she can get away for the evening. From all accounts Don Juan should find her presence at the party an enticement.'

Yvain met the playful blue eyes and realized that she could no longer keep the Graysons from meeting her guardian. 'He won't refuse,' she said, 'if Raquel is coming.'

'Then I'll send him a formal invitation right this minute.' Bettina Grayson hurried happily away to her cabin to write the invitation, and Yvain leaned over the deck rail and studied the water that could look so calm and yet hold the deeps of never-come-back.

'Is it true what people say?' Kent spoke softly above her auburn head. 'Has the elegant Raquel ambitions to be a *marquesa?*'

'Don't you think she would be perfect?' Yvain kept her gaze on the water. 'She's beautiful and she can be very gracious. She should make the ideal mistress of a castle, the most charming and witty hostess.'

'Surely a man is entitled to a little more than that?' Kent's hand touched Yvain's hair. 'Surely even an aloof *hidalgo* wants to be loved with passion?'

'Don't you think Raquel is passionate?'

'About as much so as a marble statue.'

'Kent, you hardly know her!'

'I know her type, honey. They aren't exclusive to Spanish islands.'

'Have you been acquainted with lots of girls, Kent?'

'A fair few,' he admitted with a laugh. 'It's something of a game in America, but like most men I know what kind of a girl I want for keeps. Have you heard that line about Helen of Troy?' "Is she worth keeping? Why, she is a pearl." A guy knows a real pearl from a cultured and Raquel is mighty cultured and lacks the glow that warms a man.'

Kent was lithe and fair-haired, his eyes as blue as the sea as he turned Yvain to face him. 'I have something I'd like to give you. I found it in a quaint little shop on the plaza, near that stone calvary. Spanish calvaries are darn realistic! That streak of the martyr in Spaniards.' He dug his hand in his pocket and drew out a twist of tissue paper. 'You've earned a present for being my guide and my model all this week.'

Yvain watched helplessly as he untwisted the paper and showed her a link bracelet agleam with tiny talismans. A ladder, a horseshoe, a cat, an apple, a heart ... there were about a dozen of them, beautiful little objects, cool and golden against her skin as she clasped the bracelet about her wrist.

'Oh, Kent!'

'Cute, isn't it?'

'You shouldn't give it to me.'

'Why ever not?' A deck light revealed the puzzled smile in his eyes. 'Girls in America expect to be given little tokens of a guy's esteem.'

'We aren't in America.' She fingered the talismans and then she smiled because it really was an irresistible gift and Kent's eyes were so kind and quizzical. She reached up impulsively to kiss his cheek. 'Many grateful thanks, Kent. I'll always love your bracelet.'

'I'd like you to feel like that about the donor.' Suddenly his arms were around her, her head was tipped back and his face went dark with shadow as his lips came down to meet her own. His lips were warm, caressing, and she accepted them with the need to discover if his kiss could make her forget everyone but him ... everything but the moment.

'Yvain ...?'

She buried her face against his shoulder, shaken by her own lack of feeling, her longing for the stormy enchantment of a love glimpsed only in a dream. Perhaps every girl had a dream that had to give way to reality?

They went ashore in the small launch and Kent escorted her to the castle. A few of the lights were on, but the sea tower stood dark against the starlight.

'The place looks rather grim,' Kent remarked, and he took her hand as if reluctant to let her enter the house of her guardian.

'That's because it's night time,' she said. 'In daylight the walls have a mellow look and the patios are bright with flowers. The sea tower looks romantic as it stands against the blue sky. Rapunzel could lean from its windows to watch for her lover.'

'Have you leaned from the windows of Don Juan's tower?' Kent's voice roughened, as if he suspected her of feelings a ward shouldn't feel for a handsome guardian.

'He works up there and he likes his privacy. I don't intrude on him, Kent, unless he invites me to.'

'But you've been alone with him in his tower?' Kent persisted.

'Once or twice. It's a rather exciting place, with panoramic views of the island.'

'He lords it up there, eh? The lion of the island in his den.'

'He doesn't prowl back and forth.' She gave a slight laugh. 'He is quite human, and rather lonely. Sometimes he's in pain with his leg, but he's proud and doesn't like people to know about the pain. Strong men don't like to admit to a weakness, do they? They are so foolish. It's weakness of character that women don't like.'

'And how much do you like the man?' Kent's fingers pressed the golden talismans against the fine bones of her wrist, hurting her a little. 'This Byronic character who lives in a castle, who walks with a limp and has a dark, handsome face? Yvain, little fool, you know as well as everyone else that it's *noblesse oblige* when a man of title thinks of marriage!'

'Do you take me for a romantic idiot?' She snatched her hand free of Kent's. 'Only in a shilling novelette would a *marqués* fall in love with a maid-companion!'

'We're talking about what *you* feel for him.'

'I feel grateful, Kent. Does it matter so much that he hasn't got white hair and a beard?'

'Yvain,' Kent gave a groan, and then a laugh, 'I guess I'm the idiot. It's just that you're so different from other girls I've known. I want to keep you that way even as I want to touch you and awaken you. I can't bear to think that anyone else ... do you understand?'

'Men may eat their cake, but girls must remain nicely frosted?'

'It's a little selfish of a guy to want that, but he does, and when he finds a girl ...'

'You want an assurance that my frosting has not yet melted?'

'Your voice is all frosty, Yvain.'

'Can you wonder?' Her fingers sought the handle of the patio door. 'Please, Kent, let me go now. Tomorrow we'll forget all this at the *fiesta*.'

'Invite me in for a nightcap?' Kent bent his head and spoke coaxingly against her ear. 'I promise to be a good boy.'

'I ... I'm tired.' This was true; all at once she felt as if her mixed emotions had worn her out.

'Poor kid,' he murmured. 'You're all mixed up, aren't you? But, honey, you've got to decide about Saturday. You've got to make a decision.'

'Let me make it tomorrow,' she pleaded. 'I promise I will.'

'You must talk it over with the Spanish guardian, eh?'

'I ... I think I must, Kent.'

'Don't let him persuade you against coming with us. After all, he was sending you away to Madrid.'

'Yes.' A cold shiver ran all the way down her spine. 'Now I'll say good night, Kent.'

'Good night, Yvain.' He carried her hand to his lips and the talismans made a jingling sound as he kissed her fingertips. 'Is that how a Spaniard does it?'

'I suppose so.'

'Has Don Juan ever kissed your hand?'

'Why should he?'

'Maybe because he's named after a guy who loved the ladies.'

'I do assure you, Kent, that my guardian loves only one lady, and he will attend your mother's party because Raquel will be there.'

'I find you much more enticing.'

'*Gracias, señor*, and now good night!' She broke free of him with a little laugh and escaped into the castle through the patio door.

'*Hasta mañana.*' There was an exasperated laugh in his voice. 'Girl out of a fairy tale!'

CHAPTER TEN

A SMILE lingered about her lips as she crossed the hall to an antique table and placed on a letter salver the party invitation to her guardian from Bettina Grayson.

He would see the envelope when he came in. He had probably spent the evening with Raquel and her father, and she would have told him that she was going to the farewell party the Graysons were giving on board their yacht, before they sailed away on Saturday. He would attend the party to be with Raquel, and he would meet Kent.

Her heart quickened as she passed by the golden room on her way to bed. She recalled the music her guardian had played to her, and she remembered the fiery anger in his eyes when he had ordered her not to treat him as if he were a doddering invalid. Tonight the golden room was in darkness and the piano was still. Don Juan was with the woman who would soon have every right to keep the castle rooms as they were, or to make changes in accord with her own personality. The lion would not interfere. He would indulge the woman who came here to make life less lonely for him.

Yvain ran up the stairs to her turret room and she hoped he had been a little less lonely while she had been here. She knew tonight that she would accept Kent's offer to sail away with him and his mother. In Madrid there might come a time when she would see Don Juan with his wife. There would be no chance of that in faraway America.

Before retiring she opened her wardrobe and took

another look at the costume she had hired for the *fiesta* tomorrow. It had a velvet crimson skirt banded at the hem with black ribbon. The little black jacket was of velvet with buttons of filigree silver and slitted sleeves to show the mass of frills on the cream blouse. Silver and coral beads were worn with the costume and she had bought several loops of these. Also a lace-edged mantilla, which she tried on in front of the mirror.

It framed her pensive face and was creamy against her auburn hair, and the lamps on her dressing-table set gleaming the little charms on the bracelet Kent had given her.

She fingered the little horseshoe, for luck. She touched the tiny apple, for temptation. She studied the little gold heart and wondered about love. Most people longed to be loved and to each individual love meant something different. It meant passion or security. Companionship instead of loneliness. Understanding, a hand to hold in sunshine or shadow.

Yvain met her own eyes in the mirror and saw reflected in them her own particular longing. '*It is love that I am seeking for. But of a beautiful, unheard-of kind.*' Yeats had written those lovely words and they expressed what Yvain longed for in her heart. A love like no other. A love that meant romance; that quickened the heart with its wonder, its fear and enchantment. A love that swept a girl off her feet and kept her forever in clouds.

'You romantic fool, Yvain!' She laughed as she said the words, but the longing didn't leave her eyes and she turned quickly away from the mirror.

She was tucked up in bed and it was late when she heard her guardian arrive home in the car. She heard the door of the car slam shut. She pictured him as he limped up the steps and into the hall of the castle. He would

pause beside the letter table. He would take up the envelope
she had put there and hold it a moment in his long fingers
before opening it. He was deliberate about such things,
almost as if he savoured the element of surprise. Leaning
a little on his ebony stick, he would read the invitation. He
would glance up slowly and his eyes would settle on a
tapestry or an ornament. He would savour their well-
known beauty as he considered the invitation from the
unknown Graysons. He would go to the party because
Raquel would be there. He might also go to satisfy his
curiosity about the American woman and her son. He
would have heard by now that his ward had been seen
around the island with Kent Grayson.

The morning of the *fiesta* dawned bright and sunny.
Yvain heard the bells ringing in the convent and in
the church down by the harbour. A holiday sound that
blended with the sunshine on the sea. In a mood that
swung between gaiety and apprehension she dressed in
her *fiesta* costume and went down to breakfast wearing
it. She had braided her hair and pinned it into a coronet,
and she paused in front of a mirror in the hall and studied
herself in the island dress.

Framed by the antique mirror she looked as if she had
stepped out of a distant century . . . and then she pressed
a hand to the leaping pulse in her throat as a tall, dark
figure loomed in the mirror behind her.

'Good morning, Yvain.' His voice sounded extra deep,
and she felt his eyes travelling over her, taking in the
creamy frills of her blouse, the velvet bodice, the long
crimson skirt. 'You look charming, *niña*. Almost a
señorita of the island. Come, we must cut you a carnation
to wear in your hair.'

He held out a hand to her and as his lean fingers closed

on hers, there ran all through her a thrill that was curiously warm and cold at the same time. As he led her out to the garden, she cast him a shy sideglance.

'Are you going to the *fiesta, señor?*' she asked.

'Of course.' He met her eyes and smiled in his subtle way. 'I rather enjoy this particular *fiesta*, which is called the Procession of Adam and Eve. It was introduced to the island long, long ago by the Galician bride of an ancestor of mine. She was homesick for the things she had left behind her and she persuaded her indulgent husband to re-create the procession, held each year in the mountains of Galicia, and now held each year on the Isla del Leon.'

'It's exciting.' Yvain caught at her long velvet skirt as they went down some wide stone steps to the sunken garden when the air was richly perfumed by the carnations that grew in such profusion, clambering over every piece of statuary and draping the walls in a tawny-pink and scarlet scented cloak.

Don Juan took a little mother-of-pearl knife from his pocket and cut the stem of a flower that still had the dew on its tawny-pink petals. He handed it to Yvain with a slight bow, and shyness gripped her and her hand shook a little as she fixed the flower in her hair.

'It's a wonderful day for a *fiesta*,' she said, and she buried her face in a cloak of carnations as if to cool its warmth. What was the matter with her? He wouldn't bite her head off when she told him that she was spending the day with Kent Grayson.

'It has been arranged that we watch the procession from the balcony of the mayor's house. It is directly on the *plaza* and the procession will pause there and the dancers will perform to the music of the band.' Don Juan directed her to take a seat at the circular table set for breakfast on the patio above the sunken garden. She was glad to sit down, for her knees felt shaky.

'Don Juan . . .'

'Yes, *niña*?' He poured orange juice from a carafe and placed a glass of it in front of her.

'I . . .' She took a sip of the juice and wished he was less kind to her this morning, less shattering in his stone-grey suit, less sure of her obedience when it came to the plans he made for her.

'You have something to tell me, Yvain?' He raised a black eyebrow, always a danger signal.

'How vivid the carnations look and smell this morning.' She smiled nervously at Luis as he placed eggs *flamenco* upon the table and a dish of crisp little kidneys. The sun glinted on the coffee pot, and she tensed again as Luis went silently away, leaving only the sound of the bells and the buzzing of the honey bees. She took a fried egg and kidneys from the chafing dish, and buttered a twist of bread without being able to look at her guardian. Why wasn't it easy to talk to him any more? Why this sense of constraint? It wasn't all on her side. He was gracious enough, but in a distant manner. Her heart turned over. It was as if he knew already that she had chosen to spend *fiesta* day with Kent Grayson.

'Yvain,' he carried his table napkin to his lips and she followed the action until she met his eyes, 'you seem nervous of me. If you wish to tell me that you have made other arrangements for the *fiesta*, then please do so. I shan't bite your head off, or lock you in the tower for the day.'

She gazed in a kind of wonderment at him. When he smiled like that she wanted only to please him, but when they arrived at the *fiesta*, Raquel would be there and she would look so stunning in her costume, so much the real *señorita*, that he would have eyes for no one else.

'I . . . I have made other plans,' she admitted nervously. 'I promised to spend the day with someone else.'

'A young man?'

'Yes.' She took a gulp of her coffee. 'I expect you've heard of the Graysons from Raquel. They're Americans and very nice and I've become rather friendly with them – I hope you don't mind?'

'These are the people who are giving a party on their yacht, eh? I understand that they depart tomorrow at noon?'

She nodded. '*Señor*, is it all right if I spend the day with Kent?'

'From all accounts, *niña*, you have been spending each day with him for the past week. I should hate to deprive him of your company today when he has to leave tomorrow.'

She caught the sardonic smile that played about her guardian's lips and she felt a sudden painful longing to tell him she was leaving the island with the Graysons. It was something she had to tell him, some time before tomorrow, so why not now? He might not look amused then. It might even hurt him a little that she chose to go so far away that they wouldn't meet again.

She was about to speak when she caught his gaze upon the bracelet Kent had given her, and which she had chosen to wear with her costume today because today she needed the talisman to bring her luck and courage.

'I have not seen that before!' His hand shot across the table and gripped her wrist. 'Is it a trinket you bought yourself?'

'Kent bought it for me—'

'I see.' His fingers gripped until she wanted to give a little cry of pain; in his eyes she saw a little flame of anger. 'You have known this young man less than a week and you accept from him a gift that in Spanish eyes is the sign of a betrothal.'

'Kent's an American, *señor*.' The talismans glittered as the sun caught them, the little apple and the heart swung together on her captive wrist. 'I don't suppose he even knows much about the courting habits of the Spanish.'

'Did you know, Yvain, that here on this island a Spaniard still gives to the girl he loves the symbolic wrist chain, so that everyone might know that he lays claim to her?'

'I've heard about slave bracelets, if you're referring to one of those.' She threw the words at him across the table, hurt and angry and frightened, and uncaring any more of what they said to each other because she could run to Kent. He would take her away and be kind to her.

'I suppose in a sense the betrothal bracelet does mean that a couple are enslaved.' The lean fingers slackened their painful grip, but still they held her captive, as did his dark eyes, with a tawny smoulder deep within them. 'That is what love is all about, my young romantic. A lover says *te quiero*, I want you. A lover's arms are not always gentle, and the woman who is unprepared for this is still a child.'

His fingers slipped to the bracelet and he examined each charm in turn. 'This young American has an eye for what is unusual and bewitching. Eve's apple I notice, and the ladder to the stars. Is it a farewell gift and not the love token I thought it?'

'An American gives a girl a ring – if he loves her.' She slipped free of her guardian's hold on her and jumped to her feet. 'I'm going now, *señor*. Kent will be waiting for me.

'Where does he wait, Yvain?' Don Juan poured himself another cup of coffee with deliberate movements of his lean hands that were so strong in dealing with a woman, so caressing when it came to music.

'We meet by the catalpa tree above the beach, where he moors the launch.'

'I see that you have chosen an appropriate trysting place.' Don Juan looked at her with the smile that seemed to soften his eyes to velvet. 'We call the catalpa the tree of heaven. Enjoy the *fiesta, niña*. I take it you will be at the farewell party on the young man's yacht?'

'Yes, *señor*.' Her fingers clenched the velvet of her skirt. 'Are you going to be there?'

'Mrs. Grayson has been kind enough to invite me. Yes, Yvain, I shall come to the party. I think I must meet these friends of yours.'

'I hope you and Raquel enjoy the *fiesta*.' She turned then and hurried away to meet Kent. The sun was warm on her hair and she could smell the scent of the carnation Don Juan had cut for her. She had meant to wear a mantilla, but it was in her room and she wanted to get away quickly from the castle. She wanted to be with Kent who was uncomplicated and so unlike a Spaniard. She wanted to lose herself at the *fiesta* with him; to laugh and be gay and not have to think about tomorrow.

There he waited, smoking a cigarette beneath the catalpa that leaned over the path to the beach. The air was filled with the tang of the sea, and she told herself it was the vivid sparkle that made her eyes sting.

She ran down the path as if in flight, and Kent's cigarette went flying as he held open his arms to catch her and hold her. 'Oh . . .' She was half laughing, breathless and a little tearful. 'Have I kept you waiting?'

'I'd wait all day,' he said extravagantly. 'You look more than ever like a girl out of a folk tale . . . Rapunzel who has managed to escape from her tower to be with her sweetheart.'

He held her and looked down into her eyes. 'Have we only today, Yvain, or have we tomorrow and all the days that come after?'

'Let's go to the *fiesta* and make the most of today.' Still she couldn't commit herself in words, though in her heart she had decided. 'We don't want to miss anything.'

In town they found that every balcony had been banked with flowers and hung with gay Spanish rugs and silken shawls, and upon them families were clustered in their *fiesta* clothes, laughing, strumming guitars, and throwing carnations to the people on the pavements below.

Fishing boats in the harbour were gaily decorated and the women and girls were clad in charming costumes of blue or crimson, and their necklaces and long earrings glittered in the sunshine as they turned their heads with flirting awareness of male admiration. Their fluttering fans of lace or silk were like wings in the air; the women were like butterflies beside the lean Spaniards in their dark suits, ruffled shirts and black, broad-rimmed hats. Some of the gayer younger men wore a scarlet or blue cummerbund, and the whiteness of their smiling teeth matched the whiteness of their shirts.

The bells of the church went on pealing above the laughter and the gay affection of the *fiesta* crowds. Children ran about holding the hoops of flowers they would try to throw over the heads of the pretty girls selected to ornament the procession of Adam and Eve. Street vendors were selling marzipan cakes, crisp *churros*, and drinks of iced *horchata*.

Yvain and her escort paused beside a stall on which the *horchata* was being sold. They clinked their glasses and watched a traditional jig danced to the music of drums, tambourines and a curious sort of bagpipes. In another corner of the *plaza* gipsies were whirling, and flower-hung carts were coming in from the hills, filled with more people in gay costume. Wicker-covered *garafas* of wine were slung over the backs of donkeys, and girls riding pillion behind handsome horsemen had flowers in their hair and the sleeves of their blouses were a mass of huge starched frills.

It was like a pageant out of the past and Yvain was entranced and eager to see everything. Kent lifted her to the high stone window-sill of one of the *plaza* houses, from which she would have a good view of the procession when it passed by. She felt his warm shoulder beneath her hand . . . and at the same time she felt a sudden compulsion to glance up at one of the flower-hung balconies of a tall *palacio* in the square.

Don Juan was there, tall and dark beside Raquel and her father. Raquel was wearing a lovely dress of pale blue lace and her glossy dark hair was covered by a white lace mantilla in which diamonds caught the sun. Yvain's heart seemed to turn over. There was a small carnation in her guardian's lapel, and Raquel looked just like a bride.

'Is that him?'

She glanced dazedly downwards into Kent's blue eyes.

'Is that the guardian, the tall *magnifico* standing beside the dazzling Doña Raquel?'

She nodded.

Kent turned again to look at Don Juan. 'Yes, he is much younger than I had thought him. He and Raquel make a striking couple . . . say, who's the other Spaniard standing a little way behind her? He's dressed like a matador!'

Yvain studied the good-looking Spaniard who was indeed dressed in matador costume. He was laughing and waving to the crowd below the balcony, and Yvain remembered what Raquel had once said . . . that she had a suitor who was a famous bullfighter, and that now and again he paid a visit to the island. Raquel had smiled, as if to add without words that he paid those visits in order to propose to her

As Yvain watched the group on the *palacio* balcony, Don Juan bent his tall head to say something to Raquel. She smiled, glanced at the matador and put a slender hand on Don Juan's sleeve. The sun flashed and burned in the diamonds of the bracelet Raquel was wearing. They were like fire against the dark, masculine sleeve.

Yvain glanced away. Only that morning at breakfast her guardian had told her that a man of the island still gave to the girl he loved a wrist chain or bracelet to let everyone know that he laid claim to her. Raquel would want diamonds because they suited her, and Don Juan would give generously to the woman to whom he said, *'Te quiero.'*

There came the sound of a band being played and a buzz of expectation ran round the *plaza*. The procession was heading this way and children were lifted on to their fathers' shoulders so they could aim their hoops of flowers. Girls danced at the young men . . . eternal Eves tempting them.

Yvain felt a touch on her wrist, fingers on her bracelet of charms, but she didn't dare to look at Kent. This *fiesta* was a celebration of love! Temptation was in the air, and something whispered that she might as well surrender now and tell him she is his to carry away from the island.

She was about to speak when someone cried out:

'Yoohoo!' It was Bettina Grayson with several friends. 'My dears, we've been looking all over for you both! Isn't this a lot of fun? They tell me we're about to see Adam and Eve!'

The procession arrived and flowers rained upon the figures of Adam and Eve, and upon their entourage of angels and dancers. What struck Yvain was that the man chosen to represent Adam was a mature man rather than a young one. The girlish Eve carried a white bouquet and a basket of oranges (believed by the people of southern countries to be the fruit of temptation) and her long white dress was utterly simple and enhanced by a golden girdle in the shape of a serpent. Her hair was encircled by a white silk ribbon. She smiled at Adam and offered him an orange from her basket. He shook his head emphatically and shot a smile at the crowd. Everyone laughed.

When Yvain again glanced up at the *palacio* balcony, the mayor and his party had gone inside. As the procession moved on, the crowd began to break up into groups. Yvain was carried off by the Graysons and their friends and the rest of the *fiesta* day passed for her in a kind of dream.

She joined in the laughter and the dancing, ate melon and sugary *churros* and let the gaiety sweep over her like a wave of forgetfulness. The hours slipped away, and when the coloured lights began to bloom along the harbour, the Graysons said it was time to make for the launch.

'There's the *Blue Dolphin!*' As they made their way down the steps of the harbour Kent caught at Yvain's arm and pointed out the yacht to her. Its strings of coloured lights had been lit and it rocked on the darkening water like some fairy craft. For a second or two Yvain was enchanted by the picture it made, and then all at once she realized that she couldn't face going aboard the yacht. She couldn't face any more people, any more music and wine, any more of her own false gaiety.

'I'm sorry, Kent!' She dragged her arm free of his and felt the charm bracelet become unclasped. She scrambled up the steps of the jetty and fought her way through the crowd thronging the harbour to see the fireworks. She heard Kent calling her name, but she ran on. She didn't look back, or pause, not even when she knocked her arm against the harbour wall. She hurried on, biting her lip with pain and feeling the bareness of her wrist from which the bracelet had been wrenched. She couldn't hear Kent's voice any more and she hoped he would forgive her for her irrational behaviour. She must be alone! The thought of having to smile and be gay for another three or four hours was more than she could bear. She wanted to feel the sea wind against her face, but not on the deck of a crowded yacht. She wanted to listen to the whisper of the surf and find a little ease for her heart that had been aching all day beneath her carefree mask.

She paused at last, breathless, and found herself alone on the beach. The lights of the town were a long way behind her, looking from this distance like a chain of diamonds. Soon the firework display would begin and she would watch it from here.

The sea breezes blew her hair back from her temples, cooling them. The stars were very bright and they cast a shimmer of silver over the sea. The beauty of the night plucked at her heart strings and she walked to the edge of the water, where it rippled in small waves and lipped the tiny stones and seashells.

All at once she longed to feel the cool caress of the water against her skin and she took off her shoes and nylons and stepped into the starlit surf. Her bare feet in the water looked like small white crabs, and her nerves felt soothed. Was she a little crazy to prefer this to dance music, wine and laughter?

All alone on the seashore when she could be aboard a fairylit yacht being made a fuss of by a blue-eyed young man. He would be annoyed that she had run away from him, and Don Juan would be angry that she was not present at the party when the glasses of wine were raised to wish him happiness with Raquel.

She fingered the bruise on her arm and stood lost in her thoughts as the waves lapped about her ankles. Her back was to the rocky shore that slanted upwards to the roadway, running from the town and growing steeper as it cut into the hills. Not many cars passed this way, but Yvain didn't hear the one that came to a halt on the far side of the road. The lights dimmed. The driver stepped out of the car and began to cross the road. Being on a slant it overlooked the beach and the girl standing bare-legged in the surf could be plainly seen. The wind played with her long hair, and she looked lonely and somehow lost.

Everything was quiet, and then a voice spoke her name. 'Yvain . . . is that you, child?'

She heard her name as if in a dream, as if for a moment she believed the sea had made the sound of it. Then slowly she turned and there on the shore above the sands stood a tall, dark figure. There was no one else who could make her pulses race as he did. No one else who dominated with a glance, beckoned without words, sensed her own needs before she realized them herself.

'Don Juan!'

She heard the scrape of his stick against rock and realized that he was coming down to her. The shore was uneven, he might hurt his leg, and suddenly she was running to him across the sands and they met with mutual anxiety, a reaching out that was wordless. His hands gripped her around the waist, her hands found his shoulders.

'It's you!'

'Yes.' She gave a husky laugh. 'Who else but your crazy ward?'

'I thought it! Who else but Yvain would go paddling all alone, the wind in her hair, not caring about parties and making her guardian anxious?'

'I hoped you wouldn't be anxious.' She looked into his eyes and saw that they were glittering. 'I thought you would have other things on your mind, tonight of all nights. Why should you give a thought to me?'

'Why indeed?' he mocked. He stroked her hair back from her eyes, and she shivered at the caress in his finger tips. 'Are you cold, child? You must be, with bare feet! Where are your shoes, and your stockings?'

'Somewhere.' She pointed vaguely along the beach. 'Won't Raquel mind that you have left the party in order to come and look for your truant ward?'

'Why should Raquel mind?' His hand was beneath her long switch of hair, cradling the nape of her neck, making her look up at him.

'She was wearing a betrothal bracelet. I saw her at the *fiesta* with you. She looked like a bride. . . .'

'Soon she will be a bride.'

A shudder ran through Yvain. She tried to pull away from him, but he held her firmly, and his face in the starlight was a lean sculpture with a lock of windblown hair across his forehead. 'Does it make you jealous to hear that Raquel is to be married? Do you wish you were in her shoes?'

'No . . . .'

'No, my little sea-urchin.' Suddenly the glitter in his eyes was one of laughter. 'Because Raquel is to marry a young matador who has pursued her so relentlessly that in the end she couldn't resist him. Did I not tell you that a Spaniard says *te quiero*? What woman can resist being wanted? Can you resist it?'

'Who wants me?' Yvain felt as weak as water in his arms. So it was the matador Raquel was marrying? Not her guardian! He was here and he was teasing her . . . as if he knew how she felt about him . . . and she was fired to temper by the amusement in his dark eyes. 'I ran away from Kent in front of his friends, and Rique found out that we spent the night of the fog alone together . . . at least he found out that I was with a man.'

'Did you not tell him that I was that man?'

'How could I? The whole island would expect you to . . . to marry me.'

'And you would not like that . . . to be married to me?'

'Don Juan . . .' Suddenly she could bear no more. 'I want to go away – please let me go!'

'And where would you go?'

'To Madrid. Or America as the companion of Mrs. Grayson.'

'She is quite a pleasant woman, but after a while you would be fetching and carrying for her, and each time her son looked at you she would get a little more jealous and in the end she would insist that you bundle up your lovely hair and hide your honey-brown eyes behind a pair of spectacles. No!' His arm was suddenly like steel around her. 'Not while I live and breathe! You stay with me, Yvain. I am honour bound to make you an honest woman, remember?'

'But no one knows . . . that it was you at the cottage

with me.'

'If you don't agree here and now to marry me, I shall see to it that the whole island knows.'

'But why . . .?' She couldn't speak for the beating of her heart.

'You are such an innocent.' He laughed low and savagely. 'Because I want you. Because for me you are all the wonder of the world. I love your faun's face, the little ways you have of coming close and then retreating from me. At first I told myself that I had no right to you because I am older, because I have this leg that makes me limp, but if I don't take you, you will drift back into servitude to some domineering woman and, *niña,* it is far more exciting to be domineered over by a man who loves you to distraction.'

'Me?' she whispered, while the earth shook.

'You, Yvain. I might even bear not being loved in return for a while, but I mean to make you love me.' And he gathered her close to him and his first lesson was a tender and lingering kiss. '*Te quiero, querida.* I want you for my companion. To hold, to cherish, for always. For a Spaniard those words are absolute.'

'But a *marqués* doesn't marry a maid.'

'This one does exactly what he wants to do.' The old note of arrogance rang in his deep voice. 'You were made to live in a castle, my Rapunzel, and the castle and I waited such a long time for you to come and brighten it with your youth and laughter. Yvain, would you condemn the Lion to be alone again?'

'Oh no!' Her arms tightened about his neck and she buried her face against his heart. 'If you want me, then I'm yours. You have no need, Don Juan, to teach me how to love. If there were times when I retreated from you, it was because I wanted so much to come close to you.'

He stroked her hair with his lean, strong fingers. 'Did you think that Raquel was about to become my bride?'

'You seemed to have so much in common.'

'Much, but never love, *niña*.' He raised her face to him and he smiled in the way that melted her heart. 'Shall we go home to our castle, *niña mia*?'

She nodded, for her heart was too full for further words. She thought of Kent, who would sail away tomorrow without her, leaving her where her heart was, where her heart longed to stay, for always. The pilgrim had come home, and home was the castle of her beloved Don Juan.

Harlequin Presents...

Choose from this great selection of exciting Harlequin Presents editions

Relive a great romance...
with Harlequin Presents

Complete and mail this coupon today!

Harlequin Reader Service

In U.S.A.
MPO Box 707
Niagara Falls, N.Y. 14302

In Canada
649 Ontario St.
Stratford, Ontario, N5A 6W2

Please send me the following Harlequin Presents novels. I am enclosing my check or money order for $1.50 for each novel ordered, plus 59¢ to cover postage and handling.

☐ 99	☒ 103	☐ 109
☐ 100	☒ 106	☐ 110
☒ 101	☐ 107	☒ 111
☒ 102	☐ 108	☒ 112

Number of novels checked @ $1.50 each = $_____

N.Y. and Ariz. residents add appropriate sales tax. $_____

Postage and handling $_____.59

TOTAL $_____

I enclose _____
(Please send check or money order. We cannot be responsible for cash sent through the mail.)

Prices subject to change without notice.

NAME _____
(Please Print)

ADDRESS _____

CITY _____

STATE/PROV. _____

ZIP/POSTAL CODE _____

Offer expires October 31, 1981

104568070